Whatever After

SUGAR AND SPICE

Read all the Whatever After books!

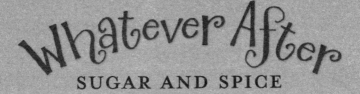

Whatever After

SUGAR AND SPICE

SARAH MLYNOWSKI

WITHDRAWN

Scholastic Inc.

This book was originally published in hardcover by Scholastic Press in 2016.

ISBN 978-0-545-85107-7

10 9 8 7 6 5 4 3 2 1   18 19 20 21 22

Printed in the U.S.A.   40

First printing 2018

for my nephew and niece,
isaac and sloane mitchell

chapter one

Lamps Can't Duck

I'm gonna get you!" Jonah says with a big grin. "I'm gonna get you!"

It's seven o'clock, we just finished dinner, and my little brother is chasing me around the living room with a ball. He's about to throw it at me, but I jump out of the way in the nick of time — ha! Go, me!

I rule at duckball.

SMASH!

I slam my eyes shut and hope for the best.

"Oopsies," Jonah says, his voice quiet.

I reopen my eyes to see that what was formerly our blue-and-white table lamp is now a pile of blue and white pieces on the wood floor.

"Jonah!" I cry. "Look what you did!"

"It wasn't my fault," he protests. "It's too dark in here. I couldn't see where I was throwing. We should have turned on the light!"

"Well, it's too late for that now, isn't it?"

This is bad. Very bad. Jonah and I are definitely not supposed to be playing duckball in the house.

Oh, you've never heard of duckball? First, let me assure you that it does not involve actual ducks in any way. It's called duckball because if you don't duck in time, you'll get hit with the ball. It's sort of like dodgeball. Exactly like dodgeball, actually. But in the story of *Aladdin*, which Jonah and I recently visited, everyone called the game "duckball" so now we do, too.

In addition to duckball, Jonah and I have learned all sorts of new stuff in the last few months. Like how to climb trees. And climb out of wells. And how to fly a magic carpet.

Yup. A magic carpet. It flew through the sky and everything. Another thing we learned in the story of *Aladdin*.

See, my brother and I found a magic mirror in our basement and it takes us into different fairy tales.

Sometimes we bring stuff back from the fairy tales, too. Like clothes. And a puppy. And the golden ball from *The Frog Prince*.

The golden ball that is right now lying next to our parents' broken lamp.

Jonah gulps. "At least the shade didn't break."

I pick up a piece of blue ceramic. "When Mom and Dad see this, they're going to —"

"When Mom and Dad see what?" my mother asks, coming up from the basement with an empty coffee mug.

Crumbs.

Since Jonah is staring at the broken lamp, my mom very quickly sees the problem.

"How many times have I told you two not to play ball in the house?" she asks. "A hundred? A thousand?"

"Probably a million," Jonah says unhelpfully.

Mom shakes her head. "Okay, cleanup time, guys. First pick up the pieces very, *very* carefully and then get the vacuum cleaner."

Uh-oh. My mother is looking at the golden ball. She's picking

3

up the golden ball. She's examining the golden ball with squinted eyes. "Hey, where did you get this?" she asks us.

I raise my eyebrows at Jonah to remind him not to say anything about *The Frog Prince*. My parents don't know that Jonah and I go into fairy tales. The fairy we met in *Snow White* told us we're not supposed to tell them. And I am very good at following instructions. Most of the time.

"I can't remember," Jonah says, plucking the golden ball out of my mother's hand.

He's probably not even lying. Jonah is only seven. I bet he'd have to think pretty hard to remember which fairy tale we got it from. Especially since we went into *The Frog Prince* two stories ago.

I know it sounds crazy, but we really *do* go into fairy tales. I'm not sure why. All I do know is that it's somehow related to Maryrose, the fairy who seems to have been cursed to live in the magic mirror in our basement. The mirror was already here when we moved into this house in Smithville. I guess Maryrose was already here, too.

How does the magic mirror work? At midnight, if we knock on it three times, it starts to hiss and swirl, and Maryrose takes us into a story. The only problem is that we don't get to choose the fairy tales. We only discover where we're going once we're there. Surprise! You're in *The Little Mermaid*! I hope you like to swim!

In case you're wondering, I do not like to swim.

"Well," my mom says, snatching the ball back from Jonah's hand, "since you're right that I've told you a million times not to play ball in the house, I'm keeping this for a while."

"But it's my favorite!" Jonah cries.

Jonah does not look happy. I'd better start vacuuming before my mom takes away TV for the rest of the night or something.

"And the two of you," Mom says, "no TV, phones, iPad, or computer for the rest of the night. None. Zippo. That way, the next time you pick up a ball in the house, you'll remember to take it outside."

Noooooo! "Mom —" I'm about to defend myself, but the expression on my mom's face tells me if I say one word, I'll lose screens for two days.

"Aww," Jonah whines.

I grab a garbage bag from under the kitchen sink and then very carefully pick up a jagged piece of broken lamp. It's kind of like the shape of Florida.

"What's all the commotion in here?" my dad asks as he comes up from the basement. He has a folder in his hands. "I can barely hear myself think." He looks over at the broken lamp. Then at me. Then at Jonah, standing with his arms crossed over his scrawny chest. He shakes his head. "Seriously?"

"Sorry," we say simultaneously.

"Come on, guys," my dad says, using his extra-stern voice. "Clean it up."

"We are!" I say, using my extra-annoyed voice.

He gives me a look. "Less attitude, Abby." My dad has been pretty stressed this week. So has my mom.

My parents are both lawyers, and when they're working on a super-important case, they get cranky. Every little thing Jonah and I do wrong is magnified a hundred and one percent.

Unfortunately, they've been on *our* case all day.

It started with the note.

At school, Ms. Masserman snapped at me, "Abby, enough!" when she caught me whispering to my best friend Robin. I had asked to borrow Robin's eraser since mine was a total nub.

6

"*You're* a total nub," Robin had teased, and I'd started laughing and she started laughing and I started laughing *really* hard and then I got in trouble.

Then Ms. Masserman caught me talking again. But this time it was because Penny, Robin's other best friend, thought the nub thing was funny, and then she started calling me a nub, which I hated because when she said it, it sounded like an insult and not a joke. So I may have told her to shut it, which Ms. Masserman overheard, and then she gave me a note about "being disrespectful in class" that I had to show to my mom and dad.

My parents were not thrilled. They told me that as punishment, I couldn't go over to my other best friend Frankie's house that evening like I'd planned. And Frankie and I were supposed to work together on a school assignment! Okay, and also play Rummy 500, a game we had both just learned and are completely obsessed with.

Then, tonight, at dinner, my parents wouldn't let me — or Jonah — have dessert until we finished our veggies.

I had to eat an entire stalk of asparagus. Do you know how

gross asparagus is? It tastes like toothpaste. And not the bubble-gum kind — the plain soapy kind. But was the asparagus enough for them? No, it wasn't! They told me I still had to eat all the spinach on my plate. Spinach! Come on. Does anyone actually like spinach? No. No one does. So I refused.

And then they didn't give us any fruitcake.

I know fruitcake isn't the world's best dessert, but it's one step above nothing. And that's what we ended up getting. Nothing.

And now — no screens!

No screens + no Frankie's house + no dessert = worst night ever.

Jonah carefully picks up another shard of lamp and puts it in the garbage bag. Meanwhile, I head to the hall closet to take out the vacuum cleaner. I'm so annoyed at my parents. What am I supposed to do when I'm done? I already finished my home-work. I guess I'll just go straight to bed.

Boring.

Our puppy, Prince — yes, the one we brought back from a fairy tale — runs up to me and paws at my leg.

"Hon," my mom says to my dad. "Let's put Prince down-stairs so he doesn't step on any lamp shards."

My dad opens the basement door. "C'mon, Prince," he says.

Prince scurries down the steps, behind my father. Our dog has been a pretty good listener lately. Last week, my dad even taught him to fetch the house keys from the kitchen table.

I turn on the vacuum cleaner. It's actually a good thing Prince is in the basement because the noise of the vacuum freaks him out. I wonder what he's doing down there.

I bite my lower lip. Hmm. What if he tries to knock on the mirror? What if that makes my dad suspicious?

I so wish my parents' home office wasn't down there. It freaks me out. They could discover our secret! Clearly, they should set their desks up in the living room and let us kids have the basement.

Plus, there are no lamps to break in the basement. There's just an overhead light.

Um, and a magic mirror.

Maybe it's best we play with the golden ball up here. Definitely don't want to risk breaking that one.

Although I wish I was in the basement going through the magic mirror right *now*.

Hmm.

I may not be able to play cards with Frankie, watch screens, or have dessert, but I know one fun thing I can do.

My mom didn't say anything about not going into fairy tales. So I wouldn't even be breaking any rules.

Right?

Right.

At 11:45 P.M., my alarm jolts me awake, and I quickly get dressed — long-sleeved T-shirt, jeans, gray-and-white hoodie, and sneakers. Then I look for my watch. I need to wear it because it keeps track of what time it is back home. Fairy tale time almost always runs much slower than Smithville time. Like one day in a fairy tale could be an hour at home.

I spot the watch sitting on top of my jewelry box and grab it. My jewelry box is amazing. It's decorated with images of fairy tale characters — but every time Jonah and I return from a story, the characters on the box change. Like Snow White, who's now wearing my old pajamas.

Unfortunately, they were my favorite pair. But what are you gonna do? You win some, you lose some, right?

I creep into Jonah's room. He leaps out of bed.

"I knew you'd want to go tonight," he says with a laugh. He's already in jeans, a sweatshirt, and his Cubs hat.

Prince, who'd been sleeping at the foot of Jonah's bed, wakes up with a tiny bark and begins wagging his tail.

"Come on, then." My brother and Prince follow me down the stairs. Prince always comes with us. He'd bark like crazy if we left him behind — and wake up our parents. No can do.

We sneak into the basement and face the magic mirror. It's bolted to the far wall. It's twice my size and has a stone frame around it that's decorated with little fairies and wings and wands. It's pretty awesome-looking. I can't believe the people who used to live here left it. Who would leave something this beautiful behind? People who have bad judgment, that's who.

I have excellent judgment. My judgment is so good that when I grow up, I'm going to be a judge. Well, first I'm going to be a lawyer, like my parents, and then I'm going to be a judge because that's the rule. But one day, I'm totally going to rock a judge robe and gavel.

"Let's do this," I say to Jonah. "It's time."

"Let me," he says, and knocks once. A hissing sound fills the room.

"Maryrose?" I call out. "It's Abby and Jonah. Are you there?"

Jonah knocks again, and the glass turns purple. He's about to knock a third time when he stops with his fist in the air. "Uh, Abby? Maybe we shouldn't go."

"Huh? What? Why?"

He twists his lower lip. "We're kind of in enough trouble. What if we get caught and Mom and Dad take my golden ball away for *a week*?"

"How would we get caught?" I ask. "We'll make sure to be home by seven in the morning when they wake us up. Or even by six forty-five when their alarm goes off. We always get home in time. Well, usually."

Jonah scrunches up his face and takes a giant step backward. Prince does, too. "I don't know," he says.

"Well, I do. Mom and Dad were mean tonight. No friends. No fun. No fruitcake. And I didn't even want fruitcake! It's the worst dessert ever! But they still wouldn't let us have it. How is that fair? They were in a bad mood and took it out on us!

12

Come on," I say. "We're going." I reach over and knock on the mirror — knock number three.

The purple swirl in the mirror widens. It feels like a vacuum sucking us in. And I should know. Tonight I am a total vacuum expert, unfortunately.

I jump through.

And something flies into my mouth.

What is that? It tastes disgusting. Bitter. Like spinach?

I spit it out. I'm flat on my belly on the ground. I push up and look around. I'm in some sort of a field that's surrounded by a blue wooden fence. Beyond the fence are huge trees. A forest. That's no surprise. We often land in forests. Fairy tales are full of forests. Fairy tales are *obsessed* with forests.

I stand and look up. The sky is pale blue with fluffy clouds, and the sun is out, but it's already lowered in the sky. I think it's late afternoon. It's a little bit chilly. Good thing Jonah and I are wearing hoodies.

And speaking of Jonah . . . um, where is he?

My eyes search the field. Instead of my brother, I see rows and rows of colorful veggies. Spinach! Cabbage! Carrots! My parents would love it here.

But I don't see Jonah. And I don't see Prince. I'm not going to worry though because this has happened before. I'm sure they'll show up any second.

Yup. Any second now.

Three. Two. One.

Okay, I'm starting to worry.

chapter two

Tweet

do not panic. *Do not panic,* I tell myself.

But did I leave Jonah and Prince behind? I *did* step through the mirror before them.

I spin around and try to figure out what I came out of.

Oh! One of the spinach patches seems to be swirling. Maybe there's still time.

I bend down and scream into the green swirl.

"Jonah! Prince! Where are you guys? Hurry up!"

Nothing happens. The swirling is slowing down. Oh, no. What if they don't come through? Should I jump back into the swirl? I've never been in a fairy tale by myself. I don't want to be in a fairy tale by myself!

Ahhhh!

I should go back in. No. Yes. No. Yes —

Suddenly, Jonah comes flying out of the patch and lands on his tush on top of a bunch of radishes.

Prince leaps out right after him, paws and legs flailing. He barks once, lands on all fours, and immediately chases after a white butterfly.

YESSSSSSS. They're here! I melt with relief.

Jonah sits up and pulls a leaf of spinach out of his mouth. "Yuck. More spinach? This stuff follows me everywhere!"

"What happened to you?" I yell. "You freaked me out!"

"What happened to *me*? That was your fault! You should have waited for us to stand closer to the mirror for the third knock! That was scary, Abby! You always hold my hand! Why didn't you hold my hand?"

Oops. I guess he's right. I was kind of overeager. "Sorry," I say sheepishly.

"It's okay." He stands and brushes bits of spinach leaves off his jeans. "I'll forgive you this time. Since we made it.

Almost didn't, but we did." He scrunches his nose and looks around. "What fairy tale are we in?" He pulls another leaf out of his hair. "Wait. These are vegetables!" His eyes light up. "Do you know what else is a vegetable? Beans! Does that mean what I hope it means? Could we finally be in *Jack and the Beanstalk*?"

Jonah always thinks we're in *Jack and the Beanstalk*. He's obsessed with *Jack and the Beanstalk*.

"I don't think beans are vegetables," I point out. "I think they're legumes or something. Or maybe fruits?"

"That's ridiculous," Jonah says with a wave of his hand. "Of course they're vegetables. So don't you think it's possible that we're in *Jack and the Beanstalk*?"

"It's possible," I say.

Jonah hops on the toes of his shoes. "It is, right? It is! We're in *Jack and the Beanstalk*! I know we are! We have to be!"

For his sake, that would be nice. I pat him on the head. "Don't get your hopes up. But let's go see."

"We should jump over the fence and look at what's outside of the field," Jonah says. He runs over to the fence and starts shouting. "Jack! Where are you? We're coming!"

I laugh. "Way to not get your hopes up."

At the fence, I bend down to give them a lift. Prince jumps over it first. Then Jonah, and then me.

"Good work," I say.

"Oh, wait," Jonah says. "Where's my Cubs hat?"

"Um . . ." I look through the fence and see it hanging lopsided over some spinach. "There."

"Let me just hop back over. Be right back." Jonah starts to climb the fence when a huge white bird flies out of nowhere and dives down toward my brother.

"Jonah!" I yell.

My brother falls back down to the ground.

The bird tweets at him angrily.

"It doesn't seem to want you to go back there," I say.

That's when I notice a sign above the field's fence. In all capital letters it says: VEGETOPIA RESIDENTS: KEEP OUT OR ELSE!

"Does that mean I can't get my Cubs cap back?" Jonah cries. "Who knows when we'll get back to Chicago? I need my hat!" We grew up near Chicago, but our new house is across the country in Smithville.

18

"Hmm. Well, technically we're not Vegetopia residents . . ." I say.

Tweet! Tweet! Tweeeeeeeet!

The massive bird honks and flaps its wings.

"But good luck explaining that to the scary bird," I add.

Jonah sighs. "Good-bye, Cubs hat. It was fun." He makes a sad face, and we turn away from the fence.

To the left of us is a pond. To the right of us is a forest.

"Let's go the forest way," I say. "I'm not in the mood to go swimming."

"You're never in the mood to go swimming," Jonah grumbles.

"To the forest!" I declare, and head into the woods. Jonah and Prince follow close behind.

This forest is dense. There are lots and lots of tall trees close together. I can hear the leaves rustling in the gentle wind, but I can't feel it.

"Let's walk until we get to something," I say.

"Like a beanstalk?" Jonah asks.

"Like anything," I say. "Something that might tell us which fairy tale we're in."

As we march through the forest, I notice that the sun is slowly lowering in the sky. It must be late afternoon. That's not good. That's never good. We need daylight. Who wants to be in a forest in the dark? Not me.

Forests have bears. And wolves. And other things that will eat us.

Who knows what could be in here? Fairy tale animals sometimes have magic powers! Really. I've met talking frogs. And talking reindeer. There could be talking lions. Or fire-breathing dragons. Or evil unicorns.

I wouldn't mind seeing a unicorn, actually. But a non-evil one, of course.

How awesome would it be to bring a unicorn back with me to Smithville? I could have a unicorn pet! Maybe it would be pink, with a sparkly horn. It would make all my friends jealous.

Penny doesn't have a pet unicorn, that's for sure.

Although I would never be able to sneak a unicorn past my parents. Especially considering how strict they've been lately.

"Abby," Jonah complains, tugging my arm, "my knee hurts. I skinned it at recess today. How much longer do we have to walk?"

I realize I've been spacing out, my mind on unicorn pets. Prince, my real pet, barks up at me, as if he can tell I've been cheating on him.

"Sorry," I say, snapping to attention. I take in our surroundings. There's just tree trunk after tree trunk. Rocks and dirt crunch beneath our sneakers. Birds twitter in the trees.

I see no unicorns. Or dragons. Or talking lions. Or even bears.

Or any sign of where we might be.

I step onto a huge rock and strain my neck to look around.

"Hey, there's another farm field with a fence around it," I say, pointing. "I think those are red peppers."

Jonah jumps on another rock. "And the sign says 'Property of Me. No Peppers for You.'"

I climb onto his rock and look for myself. The sign really does say that.

"Like I'd want a pepper," Jonah says, shaking his head. "Who steals red peppers? It's not red velvet cake. Or red licorice. Oh! Speaking of which, guess what I have?"

"What?"

He digs into his jeans pocket and pulls out an unwrapped crusty-looking lollipop. "A lollipop!"

"That looks gross, Jonah."

Prince barks. I hope he won't try to eat it.

"It's perfectly fine!" Jonah protests. "I found it in my sock drawer. And since we didn't have dessert, I thought we might want something sweet."

"I'll pass. Thanks."

"Okay, fancy-pants. Your lollipops always have to have wrappers? Do you also refuse to eat food off the floor?"

"Yes, I do."

He shrugs. "Your loss."

"Let's keep walking," I say with a sigh. "Maybe we'll spot a castle."

"Or a beanstalk."

"Or a beanstalk," I say. It's not looking *totally* unlikely at this point. "I'm sure we'll find something eventually."

There have to be houses or a town or people somewhere in Vegetopia. Someone wrote those signs. The peppers don't know how to use a pen.

We jump off the rock and zigzag around more trees. Prince begins to whine, so Jonah scoops him up.

"Um, Abby?" Jonah says. "What if we never find our way out?"

"It hasn't been that long," I say. "We only got here around an hour ago." I glance at my watch to check. Hmm. It's 2:00 A.M. back in Smithville. We left at midnight. That means we've been gone for two Smithville hours. But time always moves faster in fairy tales than it does back home. Or at least it moves at the same pace. Until now?

"Time might be slower here," I say, suddenly worried. "We need to figure out why we're here quickly and then get home."

"What do you mean, figure out why we're here?" Jonah asks. "We're here because you were mad at Mom and Dad and wanted to go through the mirror."

"Right," I say. "But why did Maryrose send us to this particular fairy tale?"

"Good question," Jonah says, pondering.

We always have a lot of questions — and very few answers.

We do know that Maryrose, the fairy in our mirror, is cursed. And we also know that she thinks we're "almost ready" for something. That's what she told us once anyway. But for what?

"We keep messing up the stories, and she keeps sending us back," I explain to Jonah, taking a wriggling Prince from his arms and setting the puppy back down on the ground. "So she must like that we change the stories. Right?"

"Or the opposite," Jonah says, kicking a pebble in front of his shoe. "Maybe she keeps sending us back *because* we keep changing them. Maybe she doesn't want us to change them. Maybe she's waiting for us to learn how to stop messing them up! And that's when she knows we're ready for our mission."

"Oh," I say. "I never thought of it like that."

I push a leafy branch out of the way, and suddenly —

BAM!

Jonah and I bump smack into a girl and a boy.

"Ouch!" I say, rubbing my forehead.

"That hurt!" says the girl, rubbing *her* forehead.

The girl and I stare at each other.

She has wavy brown hair and pale skin and looks a lot like me.

24

Like identical to me.

The boy has brown hair, pale skin, and looks a lot like Jonah. Like identical to Jonah.

I love my little brother, but the world does *not* need two of them.

The girl has a totally freaked-out expression on her face. The boy has a this-is-awesome expression on his face.

Jonah has a this-is-awesome expression on his face, too.

I can't see my own expression, but I can pretty much guess it mirrors the girl's.

"What the what?" asks the boy.

Jonah raises a hand slowly.

The boy raises a hand slowly.

I take a step back. So does the girl.

"AHHHH!" all four of us shriek.

chapter three

Mirror, Mirror in the Forest

re we looking in a mirror? Did someone put a giant mirror in the middle of the forest?

No. Clearly not. Mirrors don't speak.

Well, sometimes they do. When they're in my basement. But still.

Jonah and I take a step to the right. Mirror-me and mirror-Jonah take a step to the left. We circle each other like cats.

"You can't be me," I tell mirror-me.

"I'm not you," she barks back. "I'm me!"

But we have the same green eyes. Same small noses. Same

heart-shaped faces. Same wavy brown hair. Her hair is definitely messier than mine, though.

Wait. The girl has a mole on her left cheek. I don't have a mole on my cheek. Do I? I feel my left cheek. Nope. No mole.

I glance at the boy. His eyebrows are bushier than Jonah's.

I start to notice other differences. The girl and the boy are both much thinner than Jonah and I are. And they're wearing different clothes. The girl has on a tattered, thin brown dress. And the boy is wearing torn brown pants that are too short for him and a ripped brown shirt.

So I guess the boy isn't mirror-Jonah.

And the girl isn't mirror-me.

Still, we could be twins.

I've always wanted a twin. How cool would that be? I could dress her in my outfits to see how I look. We could pretend to be each other! We would totally share a room and have a bunk bed.

She better let me sleep on top.

Behind me, Prince lets out a frightened bark. He cowers behind my legs, clearly as freaked out as Jonah and I are at seeing our doubles here in the forest. You think he'd just be relieved *he* doesn't have a twin.

"Who *are* you guys?" I ask the boy and girl at last.

The girl looks at us suspiciously. "I'm Gretel," she says.

Gretel?

Gretel?!

Her name is Gretel? Oh! Oh! Oh! There is only one Gretel!

"Jonah!" I say. "This is Gretel!"

"Uh, hi?" Jonah says. He raises one eyebrow at me questioningly. "Nice to meet you," he tells the girl.

"Doesn't that name ring a bell?" I ask, staring at him. Come on, Jonah. How could he not know instantly who Gretel is? "Hansel and . . ." I prompt.

The boy crosses his arms in front of his chest. "Hey, how do you know my name?"

Jonah's face falls. "No! You're not Hansel! Your name is Jack! Jack, I tell you! JACK!"

"Sorry, bud," I say, and squeeze Jonah's shoulder. "We're in *Hansel and Gretel*."

"Nooooo!" Jonah says, smacking his forehead. "We were so close!"

The girl and boy turn to look at each other — their expressions saying loud and clear that they think we're totally cuckoo.

"Do you know our stepmother?" Hansel asks, hiding behind Gretel. "Is that how you know our names? Are you here to hurt us?"

"No," I assure him. "We don't know her. We swear. We must have heard your names somewhere else. Hansel and Gretel," I repeat. "The names just go together. Like peanut butter and jelly."

"Or French fries and ketchup," Jonah says. "Or ketchup and basically everything."

"Right." I put out my hand. "I'm Abby, and this is my brother, Jonah." Prince peeks out from behind my leg. "And this is our dog, Prince."

"Hi," Gretel says.

Hansel steps forward, no longer looking as fearful. "Hi."

Jonah tilts his head, eyeing Hansel, who's much shorter than Gretel.

"I thought Hansel was the older one," Jonah says.

"I thought so, too," I say. Guess not. And why did I think Hansel and Gretel were blond?

"I'm ten," Gretel says.

"Me too," I say.

"I'm seven," Hansel says.

Jonah lifts his hand for a high five. "Me too!"

Hansel stares at Jonah's hand, unsure what to do.

"Just slap it," Jonah says.

Hansel hesitates but finally does it.

"There you go!" Jonah says.

We all stare at one another for a few more seconds. It's extremely strange to run into kids who look exactly like you. Especially when those kids are Hansel and Gretel. *The* Hansel and Gretel.

"Why are you hanging out in the forest?" Jonah asks them.

"Our father and stepmother brought us out here," Gretel says. "They told us we should light a fire. But we're pretty sure they're just going to leave us in the forest like they did last time."

"They left you in the forest?" Jonah asks incredulously.

It's true. They did. I know this part of the original story, since I've read it a million times, and our nana told it to me and Jonah when we were younger. But Jonah probably doesn't remember it. I'll have to fill him in when we have some privacy.

Gretel sighs. "Last time they brought us out here, we left little pebbles along the way. When the moon shone, we followed them all the way home. But this time, we didn't have any pebbles, so my brother dropped bread crumbs as we walked. Just in case."

"I did," Hansel says proudly, in a way that reminds me of Jonah.

"Our dad told us to stay here while he and our stepmom cut some wood," Gretel continues, "only that was a few hours ago. We were going to rest a little and wait until nighttime, but . . ." Her voice trembles. "I don't think they're coming back."

Hansel kicks a rock with his shoe. "I don't think so, either."

Since I know the whole story, I *know* they're not coming back.

"You should go look for the bread crumbs now," Jonah says.

I give my brother a look. If Hansel and Gretel find their way back home now, it's totally going to mess up the story. And what if Jonah was right? What if Maryrose doesn't want us to mess up the stories? Maybe only when we leave the stories as is will Maryrose think we're ready for our real mission. Whatever that may be.

"Good idea!" Gretel cheers.

"This way," Hansel says. "I remember that tree with the half-broken limb." He points, and we follow.

"I remember that tree, too," Jonah says. "But I didn't see any bread crumbs."

Gretel bites her lip. "I'm sure we'll see the trail just past that big rock."

"Nope," Jonah says. "I had my eyes on that path so I wouldn't trip. I already skinned my knee at recess today, and I don't want to do that again. There was blood everywhere!"

"What's recess?" Hansel asks.

"Can we please talk about this later?" Gretel says, hands on her hips. "We have to find the trail of bread crumbs and get home!"

Wow, she IS just like me. Just as bossy anyway.

Hansel and Gretel rush ahead to find the trail of bread crumbs.

"They might not find them," I whisper to Jonah. "Because of the birds."

"WHAT BIRDS?" Jonah whisper-yells.

"Shhh. Okay, I'll tell you the whole story."

chapter four

Once Upon a Time

I make sure that Hansel and Gretel are out of earshot. I can see them up ahead, looking at the ground. Prince is trotting along behind me and Jonah, clearly still wary of the newcomers. "Once upon a time," I start, "there were two kids named Hansel and Gretel."

Jonah nods. "That part I got."

"Good. Anyway, Hansel and Gretel lived with their father and their mean stepmother in a small cottage in the forest. They were very poor. One day, because they were running out of food, their stepmother convinced their father to send Hansel and Gretel away. She thought the kids were too expensive and she and the dad would be more likely to survive with fewer mouths to feed. Although their father loved them, he agreed."

"Our dad wouldn't agree to that," Jonah says.

"And our mom wouldn't suggest it," I point out.

"Abby?" Jonah asks.

"Yeah?"

"How could they run out of food if there are vegetable fields all over the place?"

Hmm. "Well, the signs all say 'Keep Out,' so the people clearly aren't allowed to take any of the vegetables. They probably get attacked by that horrible bird if they try."

"Oh, right," he says. "I wonder who owns the farms."

"No idea," I say. "Now back to the story. Hansel and Gretel heard their stepmother say she planned to abandon them deep in the forest. So, as they just told us, Hansel came up with the idea of leaving little white pebbles as they walked."

"I would not want to be left out here by myself," Jonah says as the treetops rustle hard in the wind. He shivers.

I nod. Me neither. "Well, because Hansel made a trail, they

found their way home. Their dad was relieved. He felt terrible about abandoning them."

"Go, Hansel and Gretel!" Jonah says, pumping his fist in the air. "But their stepmother must have been M-A-D."

"Oh, she was," I say. "And the next time there was a food shortage, the stepmom convinced the dad that they had to lose them in the forest again. But this time, Hansel couldn't find any pebbles. The stepmother gave them one piece of bread to have for lunch, and then the parents led them into the woods. So Hansel decided to make a trail of bread crumbs by dropping little pieces of bread along the way."

"Are those the bread crumbs Hansel is looking for now?" Jonah asks, nodding up ahead. Hansel and Gretel are still examining the dirt.

"Yes," I say. "Except Hansel forgot that there are lots of birds in forests. And birds eat bread. When Hansel and Gretel wake up in the middle of the night to look for the trail, the bread crumbs are all gone."

"But it's not the middle of the night," Jonah says, looking up at the still-light sky. "So maybe the bread crumbs could still be there now?"

"It's possible," I say, biting my thumbnail. "But then we've messed up the story."

"Why, what's supposed to happen?"

"Well, after they can't find the bread crumbs, Hansel and Gretel walk and walk, deeper into the woods. They're cold and scared and hungry. But then, all of a sudden, they hear a beautiful white snowbird singing. The bird is sitting on a branch, and then it starts flying. So they follow it."

"Where does it lead them?" Jonah asks.

"To a house in the woods," I say. "Made of cake!"

"What? There are no houses made of cake," Jonah insists.

"This one is," I say. "It's made of cake and candy and gingerbread. You can eat the house!"

Jonah licks his lips. "I would totally eat that house."

My stomach growls. I would totally eat that house, too. Not that it would be safe to do so.

"Hansel and Gretel are so happy to see the cake house," I continue, "that they gobble up pieces of the roof and windowpanes. But then a woman comes out."

"Is it the stepmother?"

"No. Another woman."

"A stranger?"

"Yes. And the stranger invites them inside for a proper meal. Hansel and Gretel are thrilled. But the woman is just pretending to be nice. She's really a witch! And she made her house out of cake to lure in kids."

"Because she doesn't have any?" Jonah asks.

"Because she wants to eat one for dinner!" I say.

Jonah gasps. "That's gross!"

"Yup. And now Hansel and Gretel are trapped in her house. The witch throws Hansel in a cage. And she tells Gretel to cook for him — to fatten him up so he'll be tasty to eat for her dinner."

"Poor Hansel!" Jonah says. "Poor Gretel!"

I nod. "Well, Gretel cooks and cooks, and soon her brother is gaining a lot of weight. But the witch can't see that for herself. She has really bad eyesight. So she asks Hansel to stick his finger through the bars of the cage so she can feel if he's fat enough to eat yet."

"And is he?" Jonah asks.

"Well, he is," I say. "But Gretel doesn't want to let the witch know that. So she comes up with a great idea. She gives Hansel a chicken bone and tells him to stick that through the cage instead of his finger."

"I get it," Jonah says. "So when Hansel sticks out the chicken bone, the witch thinks that's his finger. His very skinny finger. His too-skinny-to-eat finger."

I nod. "But the witch is getting impatient. She wants Hansel fattened up fast. So the next day, the witch tells Gretel it's time to bake dough for kid pie."

"Kid pie?" Jonah shrieks. His eyes bug out.

"Yes," I say. "The witch plans to trap Gretel in the oven. But Gretel manages to trap the witch in the oven instead. Gretel frees her brother from the cage, and they take some jewels from the witch's house and run as far away as they can."

"Do they go straight home?" Jonah asks.

"No," I say. "There's this pond, and a duck has to carry them across. But then they finally get to their father's house. And he's happy to see them."

"Yeah!" Jonah pumps another fist into the air. "I'll bet their stepmother wasn't, though."

"Well, in the time Hansel and Gretel were gone, the stepmother died."

"Huh? She did? From what?"

"Um, I don't know. The story doesn't say. Hunger maybe?"

"Or maybe she got eaten by a wolf. That happens in forests, you know."

I look around and shudder. "Thanks for the reminder."

"Well, I'm glad they got home," Jonah says.

"Me too," I say.

"Oh, no!" Gretel says up ahead. She comes running back to us, Hansel behind her.

Her face is pale. "The bread crumbs are gone!" she cries.

Um, yep. I so called that. At least we didn't mess up the story.

"Did YOU eat the bread crumbs?" Hansel asks, narrowing his eyes at Jonah. "You did, didn't you?"

"My brother wouldn't eat food off the ground!" I yell. Then I remember his lollipop comment earlier, and try again. "My brother wouldn't eat bread crumbs off the ground!"

"Yeah, why would I eat bread crumbs from the dirt?" Jonah asks. "That's gross."

"Maybe your dog did it," Gretel says, glaring at Prince.

"Prince doesn't like bread," Jonah answers, bending down to

pat Prince's head. "He likes cheese. Cheese crumbs he would have gone for."

"It was probably the birds," I offer.

It was one hundred percent the birds.

"Oh, yeah," Gretel says, looking up. "The birds. We forgot about the birds."

"But now we'll never find our way home!" Hansel says, his eyes filling with tears.

Gretel wraps her arms around him and pats him on the back.

"What do we do?" Jonah whispers to me.

I glance at my watch. Oh, wow. It's 3:11 A.M. in Smithville. Time is definitely passing much slower here than it is at home. I'm pretty sure it's passing twice as slow. But how can I check? I guess I can count. "Quiet for a second, 'kay?" I tell my brother. "I need to check something." When my watch changes to three twelve, I start to count. One Mississippi, two Mississippi, three Mississippi . . . When I reach thirty, my watch changes to three thirteen. So I'm definitely right. One minute at home is thirty seconds here. Every half hour here is an hour at home. That means my parents will be up in less than four Smithville hours, which is only two hours here. AHHHH!

"I think we need to send them off to the witch's house and then start looking for the portal home," I whisper to Jonah.

"Isn't it bad to send them to the witch?" Jonah whispers back.

"I don't think so," I say nervously. "At least we know they outsmart her. And then they get her jewels and live happily ever after."

"True," Jonah says. "Can we walk with them until they get there at least? Maybe we'll get to see the cake house!" He leans closer to me. "And taste it?"

I consider. "We'll have to assess the situation. But . . . maybe one teensy piece of roof won't hurt anything."

Don't we deserve it? Our parents did make us miss dessert.

And I bet the cake house is much, much yummier than a measly piece of fruitcake.

chapter five

There Are No Lightsabers in Vegetopia

gretel is still comforting her brother.

"Don't worry," I say.

"Will you help us find our way home?" she asks.

"We'll help you," I say. But what I really mean is we'll help them find the cake house, and not their actual house.

"But how?" Gretel asks, narrowing her eyes at me and taking her brother's hand. "I would like to know a specific plan."

Why am I not surprised? I also like to always know a specific plan. Too bad I don't have one right now.

"Let's walk . . . that way," I say, pointing forward. In the original story, a bird shows them the way to the cake house. So all we have to do is find the bird.

Hmm. I hope that bird isn't the same bird that protected the fence. No, it can't be. This bird tries to help the kids, right?

I look up in the air. There are a lot of birds. But none of them are tweeting at us.

"So where are you from, anyway?" Gretel asks. "Are your parents worried about you being out in the forest by yourselves? Or did they drop you off here, like ours did?"

"Neither," I say.

Jonah snort-laughs. "Right now, our parents are so mad at us, they probably *would* drop us off here."

"Do you get in trouble a lot?" Hansel asks Jonah. "We do. Yesterday we got in trouble for not bringing in enough firewood. Our stepmom is always mad at us about something."

"Oh, we get in trouble all the time," Jonah says, nodding. "If I don't put away my toys? My parents flip. My mother took away my golden ball just because I broke a lamp! And so what if I leave my remote-controlled robot on the living room rug? Big deal, right? And I wasn't allowed to get a new lightsaber after I left mine in the yard and it got ruined by the rain." He shakes his head. "It wasn't my fault it rained!"

Hansel stops walking. "A remote what? And what's a lightsaber?"

"I guess you haven't seen *Star Wars*," Jonah says.

As Jonah tells Hansel all about his toys, I check my watch again. Another nineteen minutes have passed at home. It's 3:30 A.M. in Smithville. We've got to move it.

"How many toys do you have?" Gretel asks Jonah.

"Lots," my brother says. That's true. Our closets are over-flowing with them.

"You too?" Gretel asks me.

"Well, I don't play with toys like I used to," I say. I feel a little uncomfortable, but I'm not sure why. "But I have a lot of fun stuff in my room. Like a jewelry box and books and Legos and arts and crafts —"

"Your room?" Gretel repeats, stopping in her tracks. "What do you mean?"

"My bedroom," I say. Has she not heard of a bedroom? "Where I sleep."

"I don't have one of those," Gretel says.

"Me neither," Hansel adds.

"You're lucky," Jonah says. "We have to clean our rooms every night before bed. And then we have to wake up early to go to school."

"What's school?" Hansel asks. "Is that where you go to buy food?"

"Uh, no," Jonah says. "We buy all our food at the supermarket. You know, huge store, tons of food. Costco is the best. They give out samples. Like little dogs-in-a-blanket."

"Pigs-in-a-blanket," I say. "Not dogs."

"They're little hot dogs! They should be called dogs-in-a-blanket!"

I roll my eyes. "I know you think so, but they're not."

"Can you answer my brother's question? What's school?" Gretel asks.

"It's where we go to learn," I say. "Math. Reading. Geography."

"We have to go for seven hours a day," Jonah says with a small groan. "All the kids go. You don't go to school?"

"No," Gretel and Hansel say simultaneously.

"We do chores all day," Hansel says. "And get in trouble from our stepmother when our dad is out."

"We got in trouble last night because we didn't finish all our vegetables," Jonah says. "And then we weren't allowed to have dessert! They make us eat our veggies every night!" He makes a face and sticks out his tongue. "Even ketchup can't make spinach taste better. Or peas."

"Nothing can," I say. I actually like some vegetables, but I hate peas. So squishy.

Gretel's mouth is open. She's staring from me to Jonah and back to me. "Wait. You get vegetables every night?"

"Of course," Jonah says. "Don't you?"

They shake their heads.

"Lucky," Hansel says.

"Lucky?" Jonah asks. "Are you kidding?"

I think about everything we've said. Everything we have. Everything they don't. My cheeks heat up. She isn't kidding. Her family is really poor. According to the original story, Hansel and Gretel were lucky to eat a small piece of bread a day. We must sound like spoiled brats. I poke my brother in the shoulder.

"I'm not kidding," Gretel says. "We never get vegetables."

"But we saw a bunch of veggie plants," Jonah says. "Who do they belong to?"

"No one knows," Gretel says. "But the fence is high and it's protected by a horrible bird."

It must be really hard to live in a town called Vegetopia with lots of vegetable fields when you can't have any vegetables.

"We are lucky," I say.

Gretel nods. "We're not. We're lost."

"You'll get home soon," I tell her. "You really will." I really hope so anyway. Where is that bird? How are we going to find the cake house?

Jonah pauses next to a tree. "Maybe I should climb it and see if I can spot the cake house?"

I give him a look. He wasn't supposed to mention the cake house! We made them think we were helping them find their way home!

"What cake house?" Gretel asks. "You know someone who bakes cakes?"

"Uh, no," I say. "We just heard there was a house made out of cake in these woods."

Gretel starts laughing. "A house made out of cake? That's the dumbest thing I've ever heard."

"No, it's the YUMMIEST thing you've heard," Jonah says.

Gretel rolls her eyes. "No, I definitely mean the dumbest. Come on."

"It's not dumb," I say. Humph. One minute, Gretel is nice, and the next she's . . . not exactly sugar sweet.

"Trust me," Gretel says, flipping her wavy brown hair behind her shoulders. "If there was a house made out of cake in these woods, my brother and I would have eaten it a long time ago."

"There would be nothing left," Hansel adds. "Not a crumb."

"We're telling you, there's a cake house," Jonah says. "Let me just give the tree a quick climb to see if I can find it." He jumps up on the tree and looks out.

"Well?" I ask.

"Don't see it," Jonah says.

"Maybe you've climbed a few too many trees and fallen on your head," Gretel snaps.

Nope, she's not that sweet at all. More like sour.

Although, maybe I'd be like that, too, if my parents abandoned me in the forest. Twice.

"It's going to get dark soon," Gretel says.

I look at the setting sun. Hmm. Maybe that's the problem. In the original story, the bird only came to them in the middle of the night. And the sun here is still setting. It's about 8 P.M. We're too early. Who knows where the bird is right now? He could be on the other side of the forest! I glance at my watch again. It's four at home. We have only ninety minutes here before our parents wake us up back home. What are we going to do?

If only I had super-vision and could see through the trees. Or super-smell. Then I could smell the cake.

Wait a second.

I don't have super-smell. But I know someone who does.

"Prince?" I say.

Ruff! Ruff!

"Jonah, take the lollipop out of your pocket and give it to Prince."

"But I'm saving it!"

"Jonah! Do it!"

"Fine," he grumbles, and takes it out. He puts it under Prince's nose.

"Smell it, Prince. Take a good sniff."

He gives it a lick.

"Good enough. Now, do you smell anything like that out here? Do you smell candy?"

He cocks his little head to the side. Then he sniffs the air. Once. Twice. Three times. He gives out a bark and sets off between two trees.

"He caught the scent!" I exclaim. "Follow that dog!"

"Gimme back that lollipop," Jonah hollers. "It's still good!"

"Jonah, Prince *licked* it."

"Yeah, so?"

"You're disgusting," I say, but toss it to him as I run.

chapter six

We Want Cake!

We've been chasing Prince for about fifteen minutes, and it's now four thirty at home. Four thirty! At this point, I can only hope that the portal home is at the cake house. Because if it's not, we're never going to make it home in time.

Right now, all we see are trees, trees, and more trees. And three more vegetable fields with even bigger signs posted on the fences surrounding them. Warning signs that read: TOUCH VEGETABLES AT YOUR OWN RISK!

"What are those anyway?" Jonah asks, pointing at the leafy green plants poking out of the ground in neat rows.

"Spinach?" I say, wrinkling my nose. "Oh, wait, no — that's kale! Mom wanted to make me a kale smoothie the other day when she was having one. Thanks, but no, thanks."

"What's a smoothie?" Gretel asks.

"It's fruit and veggies and ice all mixed together. Usually they're good but not when they have kale in them."

"I've never had kale," she says wistfully.

"Where's the cake house?" Hansel demands. "I want cake!"

I'm beginning to wonder if we'll ever find the cake house. Maybe Prince isn't tracking the scent after all.

"I'm tired," Gretel complains, frowning. "Your dumb dog is leading us on a wild dog chase."

"Yeah," Hansel says. He picks up a rock and tosses it at Prince, just missing.

"Hey!" I shout.

"So?" Hansel says. "It's just a dog."

"Just a dog?" I say. "What's wrong with you? And he's not dumb. Be nice to him!"

Gretel puts her hands on her hips. "Don't tell my brother what to do!"

Ugh. I swear I don't remember Hansel and Gretel being this awful in the original story.

Jonah and I aren't this awful, are we?

No. We can't be.

Maybe they're just really hungry. Who knows when the last meal they had was? Pieces of bread are not a meal. I can't blame them for not being in the best mood.

But . . . being hungry is not an excuse to throw rocks at dogs.

"Abby," Jonah says, pointing. "Look! A house!"

Up ahead, through some trees, is a totally adorable cottage. It's light pink with a light-brown roof. The windows are trimmed in red and white.

"That's not *our* house," Gretel says. "Our house is half the size and mud brown." She stares at the cottage. "The doorknob looks like a cookie. I'm so hungry my eyes must be playing tricks on me."

It does look like a cookie. A chocolate-chip cookie. And the trim around the strawberry-colored door looks like pie crust.

Because it *is* a chocolate-chip cookie. And it *is* a pie crust. It's the cake house!

We found it! I bend down and scratch behind my dog's ears. Good job, Prince!

Jonah lifts his nose and sniffs the air. "Do you smell strawberry shortcake?" he asks.

"And brownies?" Hansel says.

"And gingerbread?" Gretel says.

"Yup, yup, and yup," I say, smiling. "You're all correct. This, my friends, is the cake house."

Gretel's eyes almost pop out of her face, slinky style. "It's real?" she asks.

"Told you so," I say smugly. Take that, Gretel!

"Hunnnnnngry," Hansel says. "Want candy."

"Me too," says Gretel. "Come on, Hansel. Let's go!"

I grin at Jonah. We're here. Whew. Now the story can unfold exactly the way it's supposed to. Yay, us.

Hansel and Gretel start running down the hill. Hansel reaches the house first.

"It smells so good," Jonah says.

"It does," I say as the yummiest-smelling breeze ever wafts toward me.

"I'm just going to run up and take a little taste. 'Kay, Abby?"

Sniff. Yum. Sniff, sniff. "But . . ."

"I don't see the witch," Jonah says. "We'll be careful. Let's just take a closer look. We have to. It's a cake house! It's THE cake house."

Well . . . we'll have to be careful . . . but . . . if the witch doesn't see us . . .

My stomach is growling.

And I could really use some dessert.

And . . . it's the CAKE HOUSE!

I run down the hill.

chapter seven

Sugar Rush

by the time we get there, Hansel has grabbed a piece of cake off the roof and stuffed it in his mouth.

"Dis is ama-ing!" he calls out, garbling his words while he chews. He grabs a handful of jelly beans decorating the front door and devours them in one gulp.

Jonah is about to do the same.

I am about to grab a scoop of cotton candy from the side of the house when my common sense comes back to me.

"Wait," I say to Jonah softly. "Let's just make sure the witch isn't watching. We *definitely* don't want her to see us eating her cake house."

"I don't think she's here," Jonah says. He peeks in through a window. "At least, I don't see anyone inside."

"Really?" I say. "Hmm. I guess it's possible that she's not home. It's not nighttime yet. The original story doesn't take place until tomorrow, so she might not even be around right now. She could be out luring children with bubble gum or something."

I take a peek through the sugary windows to be sure.

The cottage isn't as incredible on the inside. In fact, it looks just like a regular house. I guess only the outside is coated in candy. The walls are white and the kitchen and living room and dining room are one big room. But in the far corner, away from the door, there's a wooden rocking chair with a green velvet cushion. In the other corner is . . .

. . . a cage?

Yeah, I think it's a cage, but it's built into the wall. It's kind of like a closet except, instead of a closet door, there are wooden slats about an inch apart. It's big. Big enough to fit two grown people, standing. This must be where the witch kept Hansel.

Beside me, Prince barks. He's sniffing around the house, his tail wagging, taking little licks as he goes.

"Yum," says Hansel as he breaks off a piece of the window frame, which happens to be made of candy cane.

"Double yum," Gretel says, her mouth full of gingerbread.

"Abby?" Jonah pleads, clasping his hands together.

"One minute," I tell him.

Still cautious, I walk around to the back of the cottage, Prince following me. I look through every window. I don't see anyone home. I notice that on the coffee table is a tray that's covered in sparkly things. Candy? No. Oh! It's jewels! The witch's jewels! That's what Hansel and Gretel take at the end of the story.

There's no movement in the house at all. And if the witch were here, wouldn't she have come out by now? There are four kids to grab. That's four potential kid pies!

She must be somewhere else.

"The window box is made out of peanut brittle!" Gretel says, breaking off a piece. "Mmm! So good!"

I look closer at the window box. The dirt is chunks of chocolate! And the stems are green licorice. And the flowers are . . . gummies?

And the flowerpots are made of Skittles.

Mmm. I love Skittles.

"This gingerbread sure is delicious," Gretel says, munching on a shingle. "Aren't you guys going to have any?"

"C'mon, Abby!" Jonah begs. "Can't we have a little?"

I look at the walls. The strawberry shortcake walls. Mmm. I love strawberry shortcake.

But I don't want my brother going nuts.

"ONE bite of ONE thing," I tell Jonah.

He grins and rips a piece of cake off the roof. "Mmmm, icing!"

I dip my finger into the strawberry shortcake and take a scoop. It's the most delicious thing I've ever tasted.

"Yuuuuuuum," I say.

I have another little bite.

One more. So good.

Ooh, are those lemon drops? I step closer to the line of little, round yellow balls dotting the windows. I pull one off and pop it in my mouth. Amazing.

I look back through the window, and I see the cage again. It's really creepy.

I start to feel a prickling down my back. Should I not have led Hansel and Gretel here? Was that a mistake? They're about to get trapped. In the original story, they escape, but what if something goes wrong this time? What if the witch wins? What if she ends up hurting them and it's all our fault? My heart starts to race.

Through the window, the jewels on the table catch the last of the sun's rays and sparkle.

Hmm.

I turn to my brother. "Maybe," I say, "we let them skip the whole being kidnapped part, and just take the witch's jewels."

Jonah's eyes widen to the size of cookies. "You want us to steal the witch's jewels?!"

"Witch's jewels?" Gretel asks, her mouth filled with taffy. "Kidnapped? Excuse me? Would you mind telling me what's going on here?"

Oops. Should probably have used my indoor voice. I guess I'll have to tell them the truth now.

"Um, see, this is a witch's cottage," I admit. "She lives here."

"A witch lives here?" Gretel shrieks.

"Yes," I say.

"Are you sure?" Hansel asks.

"Yes," I say. "We lied to you before. We're sorry. We shouldn't have. But see, the witch is going to pretend to be nice and trap you. Eventually, you trick her and save yourselves and take her jewels . . . but you're supposed to be stuck here for a few days."

"But how do you know all that?" Gretel asks.

"It's in the story," Jonah says. "We were trying to keep it the same. But now Abby thinks you should take the jewels and just go home."

"What story?" Gretel cries. "What are you talking about? Who are you, anyway? And what do you mean *just go home*? Of course we want to *just go home*! We would if we knew how to find it!"

"Plus, I don't think it's right to steal the witch's jewels," Jonah says. "That seems wrong."

"I know it sounds wrong," I say. "But it's better than what happens to her in the original story, isn't it? And then Hansel and Gretel can get their happily-ever-after right away. They'll have enough money to buy all the food they need!"

"Yeah but . . ."

Ruff! Prince barks. *Ruff!*

61

"Yummy, huh, Prince? But remember, no chocolate."
Chocolate is totally bad for dogs. It hurts their tummies.

Ruff! Ruff-ruff!

I glance over to see where Prince is. He's not even begging
for candy. He's a few feet away from the cottage, his paw up
against a tree.

Ruff! he barks again.

Huh? Why would Prince be standing against a tree and
barking like crazy? There's no one behind it. There's no one else
around.

I walk over and look up at the tree. No squirrel. No one hiding in the leaves. So what's going on with Prince?

"What's wrong?" I ask Prince.

Ruff! Ruff-ruff! RUFFFFF! Prince barks.

"He's trying to tell us something," Jonah says.

I step even closer and stare at the tree. Hey, wait a sec. It does
look a little different from all the other trees. But what is it? The
trunk is made of brown bark and the long branches are full of big
green leaves. It's just a regular old tree.

I step closer to the tree and touch it. It feels different. Almost
like the wind is making the trunk shake a little.

Jonah rushes over. "Abby, the tree is vibrating. I mean, the center of the trunk is vibrating."

Huh? Why would —

I gasp. It's the portal! "Yay!" I look at my watch. "That's good timing. It's five in the morning at home! We only have an hour left here, and we already found the portal!"

"I'll bet you're right," Jonah says. Then he reaches over and knocks on the tree.

"Wait, Jonah!" I cry. "We can't go home just yet. We have to make sure Hansel and Gretel will be okay first. Let's get the jewels, and then we can go."

"Oops," Jonah says. "Sorry."

The tree trunk starts to swirl. Purple sparks come off it.

It's definitely the portal. But we can't leave yet!

Hansel and Gretel's eyes are both wide. They stare at the swirling purple haze in the middle of the tree trunk.

"That's how you get to your house?" Gretel asks.

"Yes," Jonah says. "When we're ready to go, we knock two more times and just jump right in."

"Does it hurt?" Hansel asks. He steps closer to the portal, peering in.

You can't see anything, though. Just purple.

"Nope," Jonah answers. "It's like walking through air."

"That's amazing," Gretel says, staring at it.

"Wow," Hansel exclaims.

It IS pretty cool. Jonah and I are so used to it that it doesn't seem like such a big deal. But I guess it is. I mean, how many kids get to jump through portals in and out of fairy tales?

"We have to tell Maryrose we're not ready to go yet," I say. "I'm sure she'll close the portal and open it when we knock again. In fifteen minutes. We'll just get the jewels first and make sure Hansel and Gretel will be okay."

"And maybe have another snack or two," Jonah adds. "Or three."

The portal is still swirling.

"Maryrose," I say to the portal, "can you just pause the swirling for like five minutes? Please?"

"Who's Maryrose?" Gretel asks.

"Oh, um, she's sort of like our travel agent," I say. "Listen, guys. We need to get the tray of jewels on the witch's coffee table. That way you'll be able to afford to buy food. Who's coming with me? Gretel?"

"Are you crazy?" Gretel asks. "I'm not going into the witch's house!"

"I'll go!" says Hansel.

Gretel puts her hand on his shoulder. "And neither is my brother," she says. "He stays with me."

Aw. She's a good sister. Just like me!

I look inside the house again. The jewels probably don't even belong to the witch. I'm sure she stole them from someone else. So I shouldn't feel bad about stealing from her. She's evil. She eats children! I'll be like Robin Hood. Taking from the rich to give to the poor. Taking from the *witch* to give to the poor.

Jonah's eyes light up. "I'll come. Sounds fun. Do you think the door is locked?"

"We could always eat through it," I say as we step closer to the entrance.

He turns the handle. "It's open!" he says with a trace of disappointment. He totally wanted to eat through the door.

I glance at my watch. "Okay, guys," I tell Hansel and Gretel. "Jonah and I are going to run inside the house. You two keep a lookout here. If you see anyone, yell out."

"Okay," Gretel says, looking at the swirling tree. I can't blame her. It's pretty cool.

Jonah carefully pushes open the door. I step forward, Prince at my heels.

I poke my head in and look around. "Hello?" I call out.

No one answers.

"Hello? Anyone home?"

Still no answer.

The witch is definitely not here. Perfect.

"Okay, let's go in. But be careful!" I tell Jonah. "We don't know much about this witch."

"Except that she likes kid pie," Jonah says.

Yeah, except that. I was trying to forget that part.

"Don't touch anything," I tell Prince. He wags his tail in understanding.

We step in farther and look around.

"I'm grabbing the jewels," I say. I run to the table and pick up the tray. "I wish I had a bag to put them in."

"Let me see if she has a plastic one under the sink," Jonah says.

I wait by the jewels and look out the front window.

Hansel and Gretel are holding hands in front of the portal.

66

Gretel looks at Hansel. She nods.

He nods back.

They both smile.

And then they go running straight for the swirling purple in the center of the tree.

"Wait!" I cry. "STOP!"

Do they wait? Do they stop? No.

They just keep going. Right into our portal home.

NOOOOO!

chapter eight

Buh-Bye!

my eyes practically pop out of my head.

No. No way did that just happen.

Except it did.

My heart speeds up, and my mouth goes dry.

Hansel and Gretel ran right into the portal. Our portal. And now they're gone.

The purple has stopped swirling. The tree looks like a normal tree.

They stole our way home! I can't believe they did that! We were being nice to them and trying to *help* them. And this is how they repay us? By stealing from us. I make fists with both my hands and slam them against my knees.

"No, no, no, NO!" I shout.

"What's wrong?" Jonah asks from where he's crouched under the witch's sink. "I still can't find a bag. Maybe Hansel and Gretel have pockets? They can stuff some of the jewels inside."

My voice comes out in a whisper. "They're gone."

"Who?"

"Hansel and Gretel," I say.

"Where'd they go?" Jonah asks, looking up with a frown. "To find a bathroom? They should probably just go behind a tree. I had to do that once with Dad when I was younger. It was an emergency, though."

"No, Jonah. They snuck into our portal."

Jonah's jaw drops. "Wait, WHAT? They went through *our portal*? But why would they do that?"

"I don't know! Because they're awful people!" I yell, feeling on the verge of tears. "Because they're thieves! What kind of people take someone else's portal?"

"We were about to take someone else's jewels," Jonah points out.

"It's not the same thing," I snap. "We were stealing from a witch! They were stealing from two little kids!"

"Who are you calling two little kids?" Jonah asks.

"Us!" I yell. "We are!"

"Abby, wait. Does that mean we're gonna be trapped in this fairy tale?" Jonah asks, biting his lip.

"No," I say quickly, although I'm unsure. "We can't be. I mean, Maryrose will know they're not us. Right?"

He bites down even harder. "How? They look just like us!"

Oh, no. My stomach tightens. That's true.

"Uh . . . uh . . ." I try to think. "She's a magic fairy. She'll be able to tell the difference."

"Are you sure?" Jonah asks.

"I'm not sure of anything right now except that Hansel and Gretel are the worst!" I yell out. I take a breath, trying to calm down. "Maybe Maryrose just trapped them in the mirror."

"Maybe," Jonah says. "Or they're . . ."

"Or they're what?" I ask.

"Or they're . . . in our house right now!"

EEK!

"We have to go after them!" I say. "Let's go knock on the portal!"

"Hurry!" Jonah says, springing to his feet. He, Prince, and I race for the door.

I reach for the doorknob.

But the door opens.

I gasp.

A woman is standing in the doorway. She's about my mom's age, maybe a little younger, and has pretty blond hair in loose waves to her shoulders. Her eyes are blue and almost the same color as her dress, which has a white lace hem. She has a big smile on her freckled face and a basket in her arms. She looks like she's selling something.

"Hello," she singsongs. "I smell children! Are there children in here?"

"Oh, um, hi," I say. "We don't live here. We were just leaving."

"Oh, I know you don't live here," she says sweetly. "I live here. You're in my house."

I take a step back.

Oh. No.

"Your house?" I ask weakly.

Prince barks, as if to say DANGER, DANGER!

"Yup!" the woman says, still smiling.

This is bad. Really, really bad. If this is her house . . . then she's the witch!

We're in her house, and she's the witch!

We've *got* to get out of here.

"We're sorry for trespassing," I say nervously, grabbing Jonah's arm. "We'll just be on our way . . ."

"No," she says, the horrible smile still plastered on her face. "You snuck into my house. You ate my candy."

"How do you know we ate your candy?" I ask.

"I can smell my strawberry shortcake on your breath!" she says with a laugh.

Oops. I lick my lips. Still good, though.

She squints at us. And she's not smiling anymore.

"Have a seat," she says coldly. "It's almost time for dinner."

I swallow, hard. I have a bad feeling about what's on the menu.

Us.

"No, thanks," I say, my voice shaking.

"That came out wrong," the witch says more softly, making her tone sweet again. "It's dinnertime. Please stay. You can have all the candy you want."

"What kind of candy?" Jonah says.

The witch smiles, revealing straight white teeth. "All kinds," she tells him. "And I'm all about sharing. My name is Patty, by the way."

"As in Peppermint Patty?" Jonah asks.

"Exactly."

"Patty," I say, "we appreciate your offer to stay for dinner, but we have to get home." I force a smile. "Come on, Jonah."

We have to get out of here. Now.

"You go to her left," I whisper to Jonah. "I'll go to her right. Go, go, go!"

We both start to run. I make it outside, but the witch grabs Jonah.

Oh, no!

Jonah!

Prince howls.

"No!" I cry. "Let my brother go."

"Let him go?" the witch repeats. "Why would I do that? He smells delicious. He'll be perfect for a stew."

Jonah's eyes widen. "I don't want to be a stew! I don't even like stew! The only time I liked it even a little bit was when Snow White made it . . . and I definitely wasn't one of the ingredients!"

Patty steps outside toward me. With one hand gripping Jonah, she grabs me with her other hand.

Wow. For someone so thin, she sure is strong. Hulk strong.

Her grip is so tight I can't get away.

"Come, kiddies," she says, dragging us back through the door. "Let's go inside."

"No!" I say. "Wait! There's a big misunderstanding!"

"Yeah!" Jonah cries. "We're not Hansel and Gretel! We just look like them!"

"Who?" the witch asks.

"Hansel and Gretel!" Jonah says. "They're the ones you were supposed to catch. But they stole our way home!"

The witch throws both of us on the floor. She uses her foot to slam the door closed. Then she stands on her tiptoes, feels for the bolt, and locks it.

She's taller than I realized. That lock is really high up. How are we ever going to get out of here?

"I don't know this Hansel and Gretel. But I'm happy to eat any children who wander near my house," she says. She looks me over. Then she eyes Jonah. "Yes, most definitely a stew," she says as if thinking out loud. "Or kid casserole of some kind?"

Kid casserole? Jonah and I look at each other and both scream, "AHHHHHH!"

Ruff! Grr-ruff! Prince barks furiously at the witch.

"What is that annoying sound?" Patty asks, peering down. "Is that a cat? Every witch needs a cat." She peers closer. "Oh, perfect! A cat! Come, darling," she says to Prince. "I have a tasty bit of spinach for you."

Hrmph? asks Prince, tilting his head to the side.

"Do you eat enough spinach?" she asks. "It's very healthy. It's a superfood."

She must have really bad eyesight. Prince is all dog.

"Maybe that's what I'll name you," Patty tells Prince. "Spinach! Or Spinny for short. Hi, Spinny! I love you, Spinny!"

Jonah and I give each other horrified looks. Spinny is officially the worst name for a dog — or a cat — ever.

Hmm. Maybe now that she thinks she has a cat, she'll let us go? Maybe all she really ever wanted was a pet?

Not that I'd leave Prince behind. No way, no how. I can't have her making a dog stew.

"Hmm," Patty says again. She's rubbing her chin. "A kid casserole sounds divine. With peas. Do I have any whole wheat noodles? I can't remember."

Please, please, please let her be out of whole wheat noodles. And non–whole wheat noodles.

She pulls both of us up. She pushes me toward the kitchen and then brings Jonah over to the cage.

"Let me go!" Jonah says.

"Why would I do that?" the witch asks.

"Because I asked nicely?" he tries. He gives her a big smile that normally works on grown-ups.

"That was asking nicely?" Patty snorts. "I don't think so. And anyway, I'm not letting you go. I've been trying to trap a kid for weeks. Now here you are. It's my lucky day."

"Is eating kids what gives you your magical powers?" Jonah asks.

"I don't have magical powers," she says. "I'm not sure who started that rumor. I think everyone just calls me a witch because of the eating-children thing."

"Then why do you have to eat kids?" I ask. "Your house is made of candy! Just eat that."

"Are you kidding me?" she asks. "I don't eat junk food. Do you know how bad that stuff is for you? I can't have that poison in my system. And anyway, I have horrible eyesight." She squints at us again. "Eating children is the only way to improve it."

"What are you talking about?" I sputter. "Eating children doesn't improve eyesight!"

She rolls her eyes. "Of course it does. Everyone knows that."

"Haven't you ever heard of carrots?" I cry. "Or glasses? Or contacts?"

"What about laser eye surgery?" Jonah asks. "I saw an ad for it at a bus stop!"

"You guys are making those things up," Patty snorts. "Everyone knows you have to eat children to see better."

This is AWFUL. Is she going to try to eat Jonah right away?

I take a deep breath. No. That's not the way the story goes. In the original tale, the witch makes Gretel cook lots and lots of food for Hansel so he gets fattened up. It takes days. So we have time.

She pinches Jonah's pinkie finger and smiles.

"Ow!" he yelps.

"Great news! You're not as scrawny as the other kids in Vegetopia," Patty says. She opens the door to the cage and shoves him inside. "In you go!" She locks it with a big black key that she puts in her dress pocket. "I hope you like it in there. I made the cage myself. The good news is, you won't have to stay here long. I can cook you tonight!"

My heart sinks as she smiles at me and adds, "Usually it takes me a week to bulk up my meals, but your brother is just right."

chapter nine

A Pail of Kale

Oh, no. Oh, no. This is not good news at all! I thought we'd have a few days! But it's true that my brother eats more than just bread crumbs! In Smithville, he'd be considered scrawny, but in Vegetopia, he's downright meaty! Ahhhh!

"Well, don't just stand there, girlie," Patty says to me. "Go turn on the oven."

"Wait. Hold up," I say, thinking fast. "You're making a huge mistake." But what kind of mistake? Must. Think. Fast! Oh! "You're making a . . . nutritional mistake."

She squints. "Excuse me?"

Yes! I got this. "I get that you're hungry. But see, my brother is like ninety-nine percent junk food. He devoured the outside of your house. He ate half the roof by himself! And besides that, he's always stuffing something sugary in his mouth. Cookies. Chocolate. Candy. I bet he has some candy hidden in his pocket right now. Go ahead, check!"

She turns to my brother. "Show me what's in your pocket," she orders.

Jonah shrugs and pulls out the mangled lollipop. "It's still good," he says.

"It is not," I say, stifling a laugh. "Prince slobbered all over it. AND it's from your sock drawer. But that's not the point, Patty. The point is, you are what you eat, right? And my brother eats *a lot* of junk food."

Patty crosses her arms in front of her chest. "You just don't want me to cook him."

"Of course I don't want you to cook him. But if you insist on cooking him, you may as well be eating something nutritious. You're the one who said junk food is poison. I get that you use your candy house to lure kids, but all the junk you get them to eat is not that good for you, now is it?"

"Hmm. I suppose not," she says.

"Exactly. Which means we need to healthen him up. Feed him some vegetables. Pump him with nutrients. Detox him. Then, by the time he's ready to be eaten, he'll be super healthy. Which will make *you* super healthy."

She nods slowly. "I like the way you think."

"I'm very smart," I say.

Jonah snorts.

I give him a dirty look. Hello! I'm trying to save his life here!

I turn back to Patty and give her one of my own special-for-grown-ups super-polite smiles. "Why don't I make him something healthy? Like a kale smoothie?"

"What's a smoothie?" Patty asks.

"Veggies, fruit, ice. They're very healthy. My mom makes them all the time when she needs a cleanse."

"All right," Patty says. "I have a lot of healthy food. Especially vegetables. See, I own all the vegetable farms in this town. My father used to own them, but after he died, they all became mine."

Wait a minute. Vegetopia. KEEP OUT signs. Fences patrolled by an evil bird. Hungry townspeople. The witch must

81

be the farmer! She's hoarding all the vegetables in Vegetopia for herself!

"Why don't you sell the vegetables at the market?" I ask.

"I sell them to the highest bidder," Patty says smugly. "Which right now means to the kings and queens in other kingdoms. They pay me in jewels. And I use the jewels to buy whatever I want. Including candy to lure kids."

"But what about the people here in Vegetopia?" I ask.

"What about them?" she snarls. "They're not my concern. It's not my problem that they can't pay my prices."

At least that explains why everyone in Vegetopia is so hungry. And it also explains where Patty got all the jewels from.

"So make yourself at home," Patty continues. "Well, a home you can't leave." She cackles. "Make yourself a kale smoothie, too, will you? And one for me. And for my kitty cat!"

Ruff! Prince barks. I think he is saying, *Please do not make me drink a kale smoothie. It sounds disgusting. Also, I'm NOT a kitty cat!*

He plops down beside the cage, his snout on his front paws. To protect Jonah! Aww.

"Good kitty!" the witch-who's-not-really-a-witch says to

Prince. "You're on guard duty. Excellent. Extra spinach for you tonight, my pet."

Prince tilts his head and eyes the witch. She leans down and gives him a pat on the head. He gives a low growl and shrinks away.

I look at Jonah. My heart totally sinks. My brother is trapped in a cage, about a day away from becoming dinner.

My heart stops. A day away? What time is it now?

I stare at my watch. It's 6:59 A.M. in Smithville. Any second now it's going to be 7:00.

Any second.

It's 7:00.

My mom and dad are awake. Right now, they are walking into our rooms and finding our beds empty.

And totally freaking out.

And where are Hansel and Gretel? Are they stuck in the magic mirror? Is Maryrose yelling at them for stealing our portal?

What's it like in the mirror anyway? Does Maryrose live there? Is there a living room? Bedrooms? Does Maryrose have a kitchen in which she makes herself coffee?

Do fairies drink coffee?

I blink. Why am I thinking about fairies and kitchens and that horrible Hansel and Gretel when my brother is in a cage! I have to get him out. I have to get us home. Right now.

I have to focus.

"I don't hear the blender!" Patty shouts.

"Uh, looking for it!" I call back.

"Top cabinet on the right," she says.

Okay, how many times have I watched my mom make Jonah and me smoothies? Strawberry and banana. Almond milk and peanut butter. Berry and orange juice. Countless times. But that doesn't mean I was paying attention. I have no idea how much to add of each ingredient. Or what to press on the blender. Oh, well. I'll just throw in some stuff and hope for the best.

I watch the witch sit down in her rocking chair and take a book from the little table beside it. She holds it so close to her face that her nose is touching the page.

"So, Patty?" Jonah calls out. "What else do you eat besides vegetables and children? Do you eat chicken?"

Is Jonah actually having a conversation with the witch? My brother will talk to anyone.

She makes a face. "I'm a vegetarian. I don't eat animals."

"But you eat children?"

"Children aren't animals," she says. "They're humans."

I'm not sure I follow her logic.

"Plus, you people taste delicious!"

"Like chicken?" Jonah asks.

"More like lollipops," she says. She admires Jonah's lollipop and then tosses it on the table.

He makes a hopeful face. "Can I have that back?"

"No," she says. "No more junk for you. From now on, you will only eat kale, spinach, and other healthy things. Good thinking, girlie."

Girlie? Oh — I guess that's me.

"Yeah, thanks, Abby," Jonah says a little sarcastically. Which is ridiculous.

"Now stop your babbling," the witch mutters. "You're distracting the girlie."

Okay, now, how to make a smoothie. I pull open the refrigerator door.

The entire fridge is full of healthy stuff. There are a ton of vegetables — everything from spinach to red and green peppers to carrots and two big purple eggplants and grapes, oranges, and berries. A bowl beside the fridge has even more healthy stuff. There are dates, raisins, peaches, and bananas.

"Make sure you add carrots!" the witch says.

Okay, here we go. I find the kale, and a banana and milk and carrots. Then I open one of the cupboards. There's oatmeal and other healthy stuff, including a container labeled FLAX-SEEDS. Perfect.

I also see two containers of whole wheat noodles.

I grab the boxes of noodles and dump them in the garbage. No noodles, no casserole, right?

"I still don't hear that blender, slowpoke!" the witch shouts.

"On it!" I say.

I reach up and take the blender out from the cabinet. I toss the food inside and throw in some ice. Now what?

Oh, look. There's a helpful button on the blender that says BLEND.

I put the top on the blender and press the button. *Whirr! Whirr-whirr!*

"Excellent, girlie!" the witch shouts over the noise.

"One healthy smoothie, coming right up!"

I take off the top of the blender. It actually looks pretty. Green and sparkly. I pour three glasses and one little bowl for Prince.

"Ready!" I say. I hand out the smoothies.

Jonah takes a sip and makes a gagging face. "Can we add some ketchup to this?"

"Absolutely not. Ketchup is pure sugar," Patty says. "I don't hear you drinking!"

Maybe Jonah could pretend to drink the smoothie and dump it somewhere? She's practically blind. But where?

I look around the cage. There's a bale of hay in the back. Is that a pail next to it?

It is!

I point to the pail and mime a spilling out motion.

Jonah's eyes light up. He rushes over and quickly pours the green drink into the pail.

He comes back over to the bars of the cage. "YUM!" he says. "This is the best smoothie I've ever had!"

"I think he'll need at least a few days of healthy food before he's ready to be eaten," I say. I'll have to sneak him some food so he doesn't starve, but I can do that. Hopefully, I'll figure out how to get us out of here faster than that.

"A few days?" Patty says. "No way. Let's speed that up. Let's give him one smoothie every hour for the next five hours or so. That should do it. Then we'll cook him."

"I don't think that's enough time to —" I begin.

"I think it is," she snaps.

Okay, then. I have five hours to figure out how to escape. I gulp.

Then I take a sip of the kale/carrot smoothie.

Ketchup wouldn't be the worst thing.

chapter ten

Jumpin' Jonahs

the witch's house is quiet. Jonah is still sitting in the cage, looking grouchy. Prince is still keeping watch outside the rails, his smoothie bowl untouched.

The witch is sitting in her rocking chair, counting her jewels. Well, squinting at them while counting them.

I try not to look at my watch, but I can't help it. It's almost nine o'clock in the morning back in Smithville. NINE O'CLOCK! What is happening at home? Have my parents called the police? School has started!

I have to get out of here. But I can't leave when Jonah is trapped in the cage. Although maybe if I sneak out I can get help?

I look over at the door — bolted way up high. The witch's eyesight is so bad that she might not see me tiptoe over and try to unlatch it. Right?

But I can't reach the lock. If only I could get to a chair. But the only chair in the room is a rocking chair, which is probably not the sturdiest. Also, it currently has a witch sitting in it.

Hmm. What about the windows? Yes! The windows!

I tiptoe over to the closest window and see if I can open it. I do my best to try to lift one, but it doesn't budge. At all. I try the others. None of them budge. Patty is not messing around. And while the outside is coated in candy, it seems like everything inside is normal house material.

And she's not letting anything in or out of this cottage. Even air.

"Girlie!" Patty cries. "Isn't it time for smoothie number two?"

Crumbs.

"Uh, yeah," I say with a sigh. "I'm on it. Maybe I should add some tomatoes and corn to the next smoothie. Did you know those are good for your eyes, too?" We had a whole nutrition unit in school last month.

"The only thing good for your eyes is children," Patty says flatly.

"That is so not true!" I say.

Many smoothies later, I'm cleaning out the blender when I hear Patty ask me, "Now how can I tell if the toxins are all out of his system?"

"I have to pee in a cup when I go to the doctor," Jonah says. "I can try that."

"That's disgusting," the witch says. "Give me your finger."

"Huh?" Jonah asks. "You're going to eat my finger?"

"No, I'm going to pinch it. To see if the toxins are out. Maybe it will be less puffy."

Oh, no. I look over at my brother. In the original story, the witch makes Hansel stick out his finger to see if he's fattening up. Gretel gives him a chicken bone to trick her, so it seems like he hasn't gained any weight and therefore isn't ready to be eaten.

But what's going to happen now? The witch is trying to make Jonah leaner! Which means I have to do the opposite.

Jonah looks exactly the same as he did when we got here. I'm not sure how three smoothies will make someone's fingers less meaty, but it was my idea so I don't point out the problem.

"Stick your finger through the bars," the witch orders Jonah.

Oh, no.

I need something that feels like a plump finger!

What do I have? Kale? Clearly no. A carrot? No. Too hard.

A fig?

Yes! A fig! I grab a fig from the fridge and run it over to my brother. I slip it between the bars and he sticks it back toward the witch.

"Here's my finger," he says.

She squeezes it. "How is that possible? Your finger is even juicier than it was before!"

Yes! It worked!

"I know what the problem is," I say.

"What?" Patty asks.

"He needs to move."

"What do you mean?"

"He's been locked in a cage for two hours. Healthy people *move*. They run. They climb. I think you should let him out and let him climb some trees. That will make him healthier for sure. It will clean out all the toxins."

Jonah gives me a thumbs-up. "I'm a very good tree climber. Even a house climber. That's how I got up on your roof!"

"I'm not letting him outside," Patty cries. "Are you crazy? But exercise is not a bad idea."

"It's not?" I ask.

She nods. "Do you know how to do a jumping jack?" she asks him.

"Of course I do," he says.

"Then do those."

"Right here? In the cage?"

"Yes! Go."

"O-kay." He starts jumping. "One. Two. Three."

At least we bought some more time.

After ten, he's just counting and not moving. Which should be fine considering the witch can barely see.

"I can't hear you jumping!" she yells.

Guess not.

"I want to feel the floor shake," she calls out. "Do it with feeling!"

He scowls. "Twelve." He jumps. "Thirteen. Fourteen —"

Poor Jonah.

A billion jumping jacks later, it's time for kale smoothie number four.

I sneak Jonah a banana, and he dumps his smoothie in the pail. He licks his lips as noisily as possible.

The witch reaches over to pinch his finger again. Luckily, Jonah sticks his finger inside the fig again just in time.

"You're not ready to eat yet," the witch groans.

Then she turns to a floor lamp and starts talking to it. "Go into the cupboard under the sink and grab me the huge piece of licorice. Maybe that will help."

Huh? Oh, she thinks the lamp is me!

"Feeding him licorice is going to help?" I ask.

"He's not going to eat it. He's going to skip rope with it!"

I find the secret junk cupboard and unfurl the longest piece of black licorice I've ever seen. It could probably be in *The Guinness Book of World Records*.

Too bad black licorice is disgusting, or I would take a bite. I hand the licorice rope to Jonah.

"Now jump!" Patty yells at him.

Inside the cage, Jonah jumps.

The witch turns back to the lamp. "Now get back in that kitchen and make me another smoothie, too! Something to tide me over! And I want him healthy in the next hour. Or I'm eating him anyway! Junky or not junky — I don't care! I'm tired and hungry, and your smoothies just aren't cutting it! They're an appetizer, but they are not a meal! Do you hear me? They are not a meal!"

"Okay," I say.

We have got to get out of here RIGHT NOW.

I go back to the kitchen.

I know now that there's no way I can leave Jonah here while I try to get help. There's no time, and there's no telling what the witch will do while I'm gone. No. The first thing I need to do is rescue Jonah from the cage. I need to get my hands on the key. But the key is in the witch's pocket.

I wonder if I can grab the key if she's distracted.

Or asleep. Yeah! It's bedtime. The sky outside is dark. It must be late.

Maybe I can help her fall asleep?

I've tried this before in another fairy tale. Where was I? What did I do? Which fairy tale involves sleep?

Oh! I remember. It was *Sleeping Beauty*. Sleeping Beauty's curse got messed up and I had to find another way to put her to sleep. I had tried singing lullabies, and then counting turtles (don't ask). The turtles worked, but how am I supposed to convince Patty to count turtles? Seems unlikely. Maybe she'll count pieces of celery. Or smoothies.

Oh! I know! I can make her fall asleep with the smoothie!

When we learned about which vegetables were good for the eyes, we also learned about foods that made you sleepy. But what were they? Warm milk, of course. But there was other stuff, too. Hmm. Some sort of nut. Oh! Almonds! And cherries! And bananas! And oatmeal! All things the witch has in the cottage.

I pour the milk in a mug and heat it up. Then, when it's warm, I blend it together with everything else, and I hand the witch the mug.

"You seem a little upset," I tell her. "This should calm you down. It's very healthy, too."

"Thank you," she says. "That's thoughtful of you. Keep jumping, boy!"

Jonah keeps jumping.

Patty sips her drink. And then she gulps it down. "This is very good," she says. "Maybe I shouldn't cook you."

"No?"

"No. I'll just eat your brother and keep you around as my personal chef."

Terrific. Who needs to be a judge? I'll just be a witch's cook.

Patty puts the cup on the table and starts rocking back and forth in the chair.

I wait. How can I hurry this along?

Maybe I should hum.

Yes. That always helps.

"Hmm," I hum softly. "Hmmmm hmmmm hmmm . . ."

Patty settles back in her chair and closes her eyes. It's working! It's working!

She sighs happily.

"Hmm, hmm, hmmm . . ." I hum. As soon as she falls asleep, I'll get the key and free Jonah from the cage, and then maybe Jonah can give me a boost up to unlock the door. It'll work. It has to.

"Why are you singing?" the witch asks.

"Um . . . 'cause I like to sing?"

"Wait a second," she says, sitting up straight. "You're singing me a lullaby! And you warmed up my milk! You're trying to get me to fall asleep, aren't you? Then you're going to try to steal the key to escape!"

"No," I say very unconvincingly.

She jumps out of the chair, and her giant bony hand grips my wrist.

"Into the cage with you!" she shouts, dragging me over. She feels around in front of her, unlocks the cage, opens the door, and throws me in, then locks it.

"But, but, but . . . who will make your smoothies?" I cry.

"Forget the smoothies," she says. "You're both going in the casserole tomorrow!"

"You can't make a casserole!" I snap. "I threw out your noodles!"

"Stew, then," she says with an evil smile.

Humph.

The witch sits down in her rocking chair. "Spinny?" she calls, looking around the room. "Where is my cat? Here, Spinny-Spinny."

Prince hurries over and curls up on the witch's lap.

I'm shocked.

Traitor!

"Good kitty," she says, her eyes closing.

I look at my watch. It's now after 1:30 P.M. back home. Are my parents in a total panic? They must be!

Is there a chance Hansel and Gretel are in our house? Maybe Maryrose let them through. Maybe she explained everything to them about how the mirror works. So then maybe they can get help! Maybe Maryrose explained everything to Hansel and Gretel and then Hansel and Gretel told our parents the whole story, and now Mom and Dad are trying to figure out how to make the mirror work so they can come rescue us.

That would mean my parents would now know the truth about the magic mirror, but given the circumstances, I am not going to worry about *that*.

Any minute now, my parents will probably come bursting through the witch's door to save us.

Any.

Minute.

Now.

Okay, now.

The door doesn't open.

WAIT.

I look over at the witch.

Her eyes are closed. She's asleep. With the key in her pocket.

The witch's snores fill the cottage.

"Jonah, she's sleeping!" I whisper.

"Finally," he says. "We need to get out of here."

"Why is Prince still sitting on her lap?" I ask, frowning.

"You mean Spinny." Jonah scrunches up his face. "Barf. Is that not the worst name you've ever heard?"

"Better than Spinach," I say. "Although, if he keeps sitting there, we'll have to change his name to Traitor."

"No! He's no traitor," Jonah tells me, nudging my arm. "Look!"

Prince is nosing around the witch's lap. I watch him ease his snout into the pocket of the witch's apron. Look what he's doing! He slowly pulls out the black key with his teeth.

Best dog ever! Go, Spinny!

"Come here, Prince!" I whisper. "Good boy! Who's the best dog? You are!" He really is good with keys.

Prince very gently jumps down and rushes over. He tries to stick his mouth between the bars, and I reach for the key. Oops. My hand collides with his nose, and the key flies out of my hands and lands on Patty's toe.

She opens her eyes and feels her front pocket.

"Are you kidding me?" Patty yells, jumping up again. "You must be kidding me."

She sniffs the air, scoops up Prince and the key, opens the cage, and throws him inside.

"Maybe Spinny will add some flavor to the stew," she snaps.

"I thought you didn't eat animals," Jonah says.

She purses her lips. "I'll make an exception."

Prince howls.

The witch sits back in the chair and stuffs the key in her pocket. "Now, can I *finally* get some sleep?"

We're doomed.

chapter eleven

Trapped

bby?" Jonah asks. "How exactly are we getting out of here?"

I plop down next to Jonah on the bale of hay on the far side of the cage.

"I don't know," I moan.

I wish I were home. I can't believe that just a few hours ago I wanted to get out of there. Now I just want to get back. I look at my watch. It's 1:45 P.M. back home. It's after lunch!

"Jonah?" I say, staring at his waist. "What are you wearing?"

"Oh," he says, looking down. "I turned the licorice into a belt. My jeans were slipping down. Mom is not going to be happy.

I think I really am losing weight in here!" The licorice has been wrapped about twenty-five times around his waist.

"No way," I say.

"Way!" he says. Then he yawns.

He puts his head down and closes his eyes.

My eyes feel heavy, too. We've been up for hours. I guess I could close them for a few minutes? It's pitch-black outside and pretty dark in here. It can't hurt to rest for just a few minutes can it . . . ?

I fell asleep! I jolt up with a start. It's still dark outside. But how long was I out for?

I glance at my watch. It's now 3:00 P.M. back home. School is done! What is happening in Smithville? Why has no one come to save us? Haven't Hansel and Gretel told my parents how they got there? Won't my parents try to find us?

Or what if Hansel and Gretel got out from someone else's mirror? What if my parents have no idea where we are? What if we're stuck here forever?

"Jonah!" I whisper-yell, shaking him awake.

"Abby?" Jonah asks.

"We fell asleep. We have to get out of here." I glance at the witch, who's thankfully still snoozing.

He nods and sits up, planting his feet on the floor. "I'm hungry. Can I eat the licorice?"

"I guess," I say. "There's also a pail of smoothie right behind you."

He makes a face. "I think I'd rather eat my belt."

"It's black licorice. Black licorice is disgusting."

"I kind of like it," he says. "I've already eaten a foot of it. But I wish I could go back outside and have more of the roof."

A lightbulb goes off in my head. "Wait a second." I turn away from Jonah and stare at the wall.

"Jonah, the wall!"

"I see it. I've been sitting next to it for hours."

"Smell it!"

He leans in closer and gives it a sniff. "It smells . . . sugary?"

"Yes! Exactly! Sugary sweet! It's a candy wall!"

"It is?"

I nod. I think it is. At least, I think I'll have to taste it to be sure. Or at least lick it. I stick out my tongue. *Please let it be candy, please let it be candy . . .*

I lick. "It tastes like candy cane," I say. "Paint doesn't taste like candy cane, does it?"

"I don't know," Jonah says. "I've never eaten paint!"

"I bet you would if it were covered in ketchup."

"Probably," he agrees.

I scrape a bit off with my fingernail and taste some more. "Do not try this at home, Jonah! Got it? But I'm like ninety-nine percent sure this is candy," I say.

"Does that mean what I think it means?" Jonah asks.

"If you're thinking that we're going to eat our way out of the cottage, then yes."

He licks his lips. "Let's do it."

We lick and bite and chew. And lick and bite and chew some more.

We each tackle a different section. I'm on one end, Jonah's on the other, and Prince is in the middle. At least he's supposed to be.

"Stay on your side," I order Prince when he accidentally slobbers all over my nose.

"I'm getting full," Jonah says. "I have to loosen my licorice belt."

The candy walls are like a foot thick. And hard. We keep at it for over an hour until our tongues are numb and Jonah looks a little green.

"I think I might barf," he says. "For real this time."

"The bucket is right behind you," I say. "The barf will blend right in. Do it quickly because I think we're almost through."

He takes a deep breath. "I think I can hold it in."

I scrape one more piece out, and I feel it. Fresh air! I look outside and see the night sky. We did it! We ate our way out of the cage! I take out another chunk and chew fast. The hole is almost big enough. So close! I can see the tree. Our portal home. It's right in front of us!

"Come on, guys. We're almost there!" I whisper. "Eat! Eat! Eat!"

We eat and eat until the hole is big enough. I lift Prince out, help Jonah through, and then shimmy through myself.

We did it! We escaped! We're free!

chapter twelve

Spinny Is the Cat's Meow

"Run for the portal!" I yell. "Run!"

Even though it's pitch-black outside, the full moon and stars are bright, so we can see where we're going.

I reach the portal first and smash my fist against it hard. Ouch. I think that was a little *too* hard.

I wait for the swirl. Or the hiss. Or some purple sparks. Even a vibration. The portals home don't always follow the same order as the mirror in our basement. C'mon swirl, c'mon!

Nothing happens. No swirl. No hiss. No purple. No vibrations. Nothing un-treelike at all.

Ahh! I hit it again, even harder.

Still nothing.

"Abby? Why isn't it working?" Jonah asks.

I stare at the tree. This is definitely the one that swirled before. So why isn't it working now?

Oh no oh no oh no.

I have a really, really, really terrible thought.

Did Maryrose think Hansel and Gretel were *us* and close the portal forever?

No. Yes. Maybe.

Ahhhhh!

How are we supposed to get home?

"This is a huge problem!" I cry. I kick the tree with the toe of my shoe. Ow.

"Let me try," Jonah says, and knocks on the tree. Once. Twice. Three times.

No go.

"Spinny!" we hear from inside the cottage. "I'm sorry I got mad at you. I miss you. Let's make up. Let me give you something yummy to eat. Do you want some kale? Where are you? I can't smell you."

Oh, terrific. Now the witch is awake. The portal isn't working, and she's awake.

"Run, guys, run!" I yell. "We have to get away!"

We bolt from the cake house into the forest, pushing branches out of our way as we go.

We hear her front door open. "Cauliflower!" the witch screeches. "Stop those kids!"

Cauliflower? I spot a beautiful snow-white bird soar through the sky. That's Cauliflower? Is that the bird we saw protecting the fields? I think it is! Oh! It's probably also the bird from the original story! The one who was supposed to bring Hansel and Gretel to the house in the first place! He — or she — must be working for the witch!

Patty is really bad at naming animals.

Suddenly, Cauliflower dives down toward Jonah.

Ah! No!!!!!

The bird grips the back of his hoodie in its beak.

"Let go!" I scream, running toward my brother. "Let go right now!"

Cauliflower flaps its wings and carries a squirming Jonah right over the trees and back toward the cake house.

"Stop!" I scream, even louder than before. Panting, I arrive right back at the house in time to see Cauliflower drop Jonah with a thud on the ground in front of Patty before flying off into the distance.

Shakily, Jonah stands up. He clutches his stomach . . . and throws up on the witch's bare feet.

I feel bad for Jonah, but I have to say, the witch kind of deserved that.

"Gross," Patty snaps.

"Sorry," Jonah says sheepishly. "Too much candy."

"Candy?" Patty says, grabbing him by the shoulders. "You were supposed to be drinking SMOOTHIES. Coming, girlie?" she adds, narrowing her ice-blue eyes at me. She tightens her grip on Jonah. "You won't leave your brother all alone, will you?"

"No," I admit.

"It's time for breakfast. Forget kid casserole. I'm making a kid omelet!"

"That's the most disgusting one yet," Jonah says. "Do you at least use ketchup with that? Omelets should always be served with ketchup."

"Are you really talking about ketchup at a time like this?" I ask. "Can we focus on the current problem? The problem being that Patty is about to cook us with a side of bacon?"

"I don't eat bacon," Patty reminds us. "I'm a vegetarian."

I snort. "Right. Sorry. No pigs. Just humans."

I take a step closer to the house, trying to think of how to get out of this.

How did Gretel get the witch in the original story?

Oh. I remember. She tricked the witch! She told her she needed help with the oven and then pushed her in.

Can I trick the witch, too? Without pushing her into an oven though, because that sounds super creepy.

I turn back toward the tree we just knocked on. It may not be a portal, but maybe it's good for something?

"Oh, no!" I cry. "Patty! Look! You have to help! Spinny ran up the tree and is stuck between two branches, and he can't get out!"

"What?" she says, looking around. "I don't see Spinny!"

"Over there!" Jonah says, starting to fake-cry. Jonah is really good at fake-crying. Usually it's annoying, but not this time. "He's stuck all the way up there. Poor Spinny!"

She sniffs the air. "Spinny! Where are you?"

Ruff! Ruff! Prince cries out from near the tree, helping me out. Good cat!

"Hurry!" I say. "Spinny is in trouble. He needs you!"

"I'm coming, Spinny!" the witch yelps. She rushes over to the tree and reaches her arms up. "Jump to me, Spinny. Jump!"

I motion to Jonah's licorice belt.

Take it off! I mouth.

I need it, he mouths back.

We need it more, I mouth, and point to the tree.

Oh! he mouths, finally getting it. He unwraps the belt one, two, twenty times from his waist. Then he tosses me one end, and we start running. Before Patty knows what's happening, Jonah and I race in opposite directions around the tree, tying her tightly to it and knotting the licorice rope around the back of the trunk.

Patty unsuccessfully tries to untie herself. "Hey! You tricked me!"

"I did!" I say. "Trust me, though — if you read the original story, you'd know it was better than what was supposed to happen to you."

Ruff! Prince barks.

"Let me out this instant!" the witch screeches.

"No can do," I say. "But you can always eat your way out."

She spits on the ground. "Black licorice? Disgusting!"

"I totally agree," I call out. I pocket some Skittles for the road and follow my brother and dog into the forest.

chapter thirteen

Daddy-O

W here are we running to?" Jonah asks.

"I'm not sure," I say. "But I want to get as far away from the witch as possible. And if you see that horrible bird, hide!"

"No kidding," he says. "Although flying with him was kind of fun."

"How was that fun? You threw up!"

"That part wasn't fun," he says. "Obviously. The before part."

"When he had his talons in your shoulders?"

"Yeah. Exactly."

"You're weird," I say. Then I have an idea. "Maybe we should go back to the vegetable patches. Remember where we came in? Maybe there's a portal there."

"Oh! Good idea! I think it was that way!" Jonah points to the left.

But Prince is running to the right. *Ruff! Ruff!*

Great. Just what I want to do. Get lost in the forest in the middle of the night.

"What's wrong with him?" I ask, looking around wildly. "He's going the wrong way! And I don't want Cauliflower to hear him! Prince, come back!"

But he keeps going. "We have to follow him," Jonah says, and bolts after our puppy.

We start running, pushing tree branches out of our way. Suddenly, I see two people — one man and one woman — standing in a clearing and looking all around. They're holding lanterns.

"They have to be here somewhere!" the man says in a frantic voice. "Hansel! Gretel! Where are you? It's Dad!"

Oh!

Their father is looking for them. His forehead is all crinkled with worry. He looks a lot like Hansel. An older Hansel. Which means he also kind of looks like an older Jonah, and a little like my dad. So weird.

I'm worried at first that the woman at his side is the evil step-mom. I notice that she's wearing a tan uniform with a tall hat. A shiny gold badge on her chest reads OFFICER GREENMONT. In the hand that's not holding the lantern, she's carrying what looks like a white slingshot.

Is she a police officer?

Ruff! Prince barks at them. *Ruff-ruff!*

Hansel and Gretel's dad looks in the direction of the barks. So does Officer Greenmont. They see us!

"Officer! There they are!" the father says, his face lighting up. "Hansel! Gretel! We found you!"

Oops. He thinks we're his kids.

The father and the policewoman run over to us.

"I'm so happy to see you!" their dad says, his voice cracking with emotion. "I'm so sorry I let Stephanie leave you here. I don't know what I was thinking. Will you ever forgive me?"

As he's about to hug us, I step back. "Wait! Sir, we're not Hansel and Gretel! I know we look like your kids, but it's not us."

"Huh?" he asks, peering at me and then at Jonah.

"My brother, Jonah? See? His eyebrows aren't as bushy as Hansel's," I point out. "And I don't have the mole Gretel has on her left cheek." I tap my cheek. "And we're not as skinny as they are."

The father lifts up his lantern, leans in closer, and studies us. "Holy moly! You're NOT Gretel," he says to me. He stares at Jonah, tilting his head left and then right. "And you're not Hansel!" His face falls. "So how do you know so much about them? And where are they?"

"It's kind of a funny story," I say. Although I'm not sure how funny he's going to find the notion of his kids going via tree to another world. "But we're pretty sure they're somewhere safe. We'll go get them and tell them to meet you back at your cottage."

"We'll come, too," the officer says, squaring her shoulders.

"They went through the —" Jonah says.

I give him a look. "No, I don't think you can. Sorry!" Imagine if the officer and Hansel and Gretel's dad went through the portal and ended up in our house, *too*? We'd lose screen time for a year.

Jonah seems to realize his mistake and says, "I promise we'll get them back to you really soon."

"And anyway," I add, "you guys need to pop by the witch's house. You know — Patty? She, um, kidnapped us and then tried to eat us. We tied her with licorice to a tree, but we're not sure how long that will hold."

"Got it," the officer says, saluting me. "Thanks, kids. We've been eyeing her for the mysterious disappearance of kids for a while. We'll take her to the station."

Hansel and Gretel's dad nods. "Please tell Hansel and Gretel that they never have to worry about Stephanie again. We're getting divorced. I can't stay with a woman who wants me to abandon my children."

"Yeah," I say, nodding. "That's probably wise." No need to go into the whole I-think-she's-about-to-die part, right?

Tweet! Tweet-tweet!

We all look up. It's the white snowbird — Cauliflower! It's flying right toward us with a gleaming, evil look in its eye.

"Everyone hide!" the policewoman calls out. "That bird is dangerous."

We all run for cover.

I grab Jonah, and we press our backs against a large tree. Prince crouches down beside us. Hansel and Gretel's dad dives behind another tree.

Officer Greenmont pulls out her slingshot and starts shooting pebbles at the bird.

She just misses.

"Ahh," she mutters. "I'm out. Does anyone have anything else I can shoot?"

Why are people in this fairy tale always running out of pebbles? Wait. I have something. I reach into my jean pockets. "Here!" I cry. "Take my Skittles!" I'll just keep one for myself. I put one in my back pocket. Two. Three, and that's it.

She grabs the rest from my hand. "Thanks!"

She shoots once, twice, three times . . .

And scores! She hits Cauliflower smack in the beak. He comes crashing to the ground, and then she throws a net over him.

There are feathers poking out of the net.

"Oh, tweet!" the bird screeches. "I can't believe you caught me!"

"I can't believe you talk!" I say.

"Why wouldn't I talk?" he asks.

"I . . . I don't know," I say. Fairy lands are weird.

"Why are you helping Patty?" the police woman asks.

"She pays me in sunflower seeds, and in return, I protect her vegetable fields and arrange the sale of her vegetables."

"Now that she's going to jail, her farms will belong to everyone," Officer Greenmont says. "Her jewels, too."

"You're the worst," Cauliflower cries. "And you can't trap me. I need to be free! I'm a bird!"

"You'll always be a bird," the officer says. "But from now on, you're going to be a jailbird."

"Hah!" Jonah laughs.

Even Hansel and Gretel's dad laughs.

The officer smiles at him.

Hmm. I wonder if she could be stepmother number two someday. A much nicer one.

I'm getting ahead of myself.

"We gotta go," I say. "We're going to get Hansel and Gretel back to you."

"Please do," the dad calls. "Tell them I'll be at the police station, waiting!"

I nod, and Jonah and I rush off toward the magic spinach patch.

chapter fourteen

Don't Duck

but instead we come to a pond. It looks calm and beautiful at night. The reflection of the moon on the water makes it look like there are two moons.

Prince barks and laps at the water.

"Was this here before?" Jonah asks. "I don't remember going for a swim."

"We went the other way, remember?" I say worriedly. We don't have time for this! I look at my watch. It's five o'clock back home. Five! O'clock! School is done! It's almost dinnertime!

"The pond is huge. It'll take an hour for us to walk around it." I can't even see the sides of the pond — that's how big it is.

"Maybe someone left a boat somewhere around here," Jonah says.

We scan the darkness for something that might float. A canoe would be good. Not that a canoe worked out so well for us in *The Frog Prince*.

But maybe there's a log . . . Or a helicopter.

"There's nothing but leaves," I cry. "And twigs. We could make a raft out of sticks."

Prince picks up a twig in his mouth and drops it at my feet. Aww. What a good cat-dog.

But seriously, how are we going to get across that pond?

"Abby, look!" Jonah cries, pointing.

"What?" I ask.

I gasp.

A large black-and-white duck with a bright yellow beak is coasting right through the watery moon and across the pond.

"Do you think it's evil?" Jonah asks.

I smile with relief. "No. It's the duck from the original story!

The one that gave Hansel and Gretel a piggyback ride — make that a duckyback ride — across the lake to their house! Hello! Ms. Duck?" I call out. "Hello?"

"Why do you think it's a girl?"

"Why wouldn't it be a girl?"

"I bet you one lollipop that it's a boy," Jonah says.

"Jonah! Did you take a lollipop on our way out?"

"I took *my* lollipop on our way out."

I snort-laugh. "I do not want your sock-drawer, Prince-licked lollipop."

"Your loss, fancy-pants."

The duck starts swimming over to us.

"Wow, that's one big duck," Jonah says as the duck reaches the shore. "I think we can all fit on its back."

"Hello there, duck," I say. "Do you think you could give us a ride across the pond? We're in a big rush."

Please, please, please don't be an evil minion working for Patty, I think.

"Sure," the duck says, and swims closer.

It talks?

It talks.

It edges sideways so we can all climb on.

"You don't work for the witch, do you?" Jonah asks before we get on the duck's feathery back.

"No," it says.

"As if it would tell you if it did," I mutter.

"Are you a girl or a boy?" Jonah asks. "Settle a bet?"

"Girl," the duck says.

"Wahoo!" I say. "Pay up."

Jonah hands over his gross lollipop. "This is going in a trash-can as soon as I see one," I tell him.

"But it's still good!"

I roll my eyes. We pile onto the duck, and Prince gets in my lap. The duck doesn't sink. In fact, she quacks a song the entire way across the pond.

"Ms. Duck, can I ask you another question?" Jonah says as she's paddling across.

"Sure," the duck responds.

"Are you good at duckball? I mean, you must be because you're a duck."

I roll my eyes.

"Well, I can't say I've ever played duckball, but I AM really good at ducking," Ms. Duck says. "Watch me!" She ducks under the water, taking us with her.

"No!" I yell as I'm pulled under.

Too late.

She pops up.

We're all soaked. Prince barks loudly.

I turn around and give my brother a dirty look.

"Sorry," he says, shaking his wet hair off his forehead. But his eyes are gleaming and he doesn't look sorry at all.

When we get to the other side, we thank Ms. Duck and slide off her back. Then we run to the fence around the vegetable fields.

We climb back over the fence. With no bird to stop us, it's easy peasy, vegetable squeasy.

I look at my watch. GAH! It's 6:45 P.M. at home! The middle of dinnertime. Our parents have to be freaking out.

We've been gone almost nineteen hours. By this point there are probably hundreds of police cars combing the streets. They've probably shown our pictures on the news.

I hope they didn't use my class picture from this year. I was not having a good hair day.

I feel a lump in my throat. Who cares about my picture? Our poor parents. They're probably really, really worried.

"This better work," I say frantically as we approach the spinach patch. "Otherwise we'll have to move in forever with Hansel and Gretel's dad."

"Are you kidding?" Jonah says. "If we stayed here, we would totally live in the candy house. It's empty!"

"Good point," I say.

We look at all the rows and rows of vegetables. There are at least a hundred rows each way, making a square. So like a thousand different patches.

"So which one did we come out of?" Jonah asks.

"I know it was a spinach patch," I say.

"Um, there are a lot of spinach patches," Jonah says, gesturing around.

I nod. "There sure are. I think it was somewhere in the middle-ish?" Oh my goodness. Are we going to have to knock on all the patches? That's going to take forever. And what if it doesn't even work?

"Wait. Abby!" Jonah says. "Let's look for my base-ball hat!"

I roll my eyes impatiently. "Of course, I want you to find your hat, Jonah. But we really have to focus on getting home. We can always get another hat."

Jonah pokes me in the side. "Yeah, but *this* hat will be sitting right where we came out. So if we find the hat . . ."

"We find the spinach patch," I finish. Duh. "Smart thinking, Jonah!"

"Thanks," he says, and smiles.

The two of us walk separately through the patches, carefully studying the ground, until my brother hollers, "Here it is! I found it! My hat!"

Prince and I run over as Jonah places the Cubs cap squarely on his wet head. He points to the patch on his left. "That's it, right, Abby?"

"I think so," I say, squeezing his shoulder. "Good job."

Prince looks at us and barks. Then he jumps on the spinach patch and smashes his paw against it.

It turns purple and starts to spin.

Oh! "Look! Maryrose is opening it for us. Wahoo!" I cry, filled with relief.

"Yes!" Jonah shrieks. "Bye, Vegetopia!"

Jonah and I hold hands. Prince is ready to jump. And on my count of three, we all leap in.

chapter fifteen

Impostors!

CLUNK!

The three of us land right on the basement floor. Home, sweet home.

I've never been so happy to see the basement of our house in my entire life.

"Should we try to talk to Maryrose?" Jonah gasps as we scramble to our feet. "To find out where Hansel and Gretel are?"

I look around the basement. It's empty. No Hansel and Gretel here.

"Let's just show our faces to Mom and Dad and make sure we're not in huge trouble or that the police aren't searching all over Smithville for us," I say.

But they must be. We've been gone *all* day.

"Right," Jonah says. "Let's go. Come on, Prince!"

Jonah and I go racing up the stairs. I hear voices coming from the kitchen. My mom and dad. Are they talking about us? Wondering where we could possibly be?

No. They're not, actually.

"I've always loved creamed spinach," my mom is saying. "Even as a kid. I could eat an entire bowl of it!"

I hear laughter.

"I was like that with mashed potatoes," my dad is saying. "I could eat two bowls full. Especially with sour cream. Mmm. I've always loved sour cream."

I stop just to the side of the kitchen doorway, out of sight. I look at Jonah and hold a finger up to my lips.

Now my dad is telling some story about getting caught feeding his Brussels sprouts to his dog when he was a kid.

Huh? Why are they talking about vegetables? Why are they laughing? Shouldn't there be a search party out looking for us?

We've been missing for almost nineteen hours! Has my horrible class picture not been featured on the nightly news?

"Abby, honey, can you pass the steak?" I hear my mom say.

Wait. What? Did she just say *Abby*? Who is she talking to? There is no way my mom can see me from where I'm standing. I inch closer to the doorway.

"Sure, Mom!" I hear a voice say. A voice that sounds a lot like mine. Except it's not my voice. Obviously.

It's GRETEL'S.

I stare at Jonah. He stares back, his eyes huge.

We peer around the edge of the doorway. My parents are sitting at the table in their usual spots.

Guess who are in *our* usual spots?

HANSEL AND GRETEL!

They're wearing our clothes.

They're eating our dinner.

They're talking to our parents.

And is it my imagination, or does Gretel's hair look exactly like mine now? She must have used my brush! And I can't see her mole. She must have covered it up with powder or something.

And Hansel's eyebrows look less bushy! Did Hansel pluck his eyebrows? What is wrong with these people?!

"Jonah!" my dad says. While looking at HANSEL.

Uh-oh. What did Hansel do? He's going to get Jonah — the real Jonah — in even more trouble.

"You ate an entire helping of spinach!" my dad says. "Awesome! And you didn't even need ketchup."

Hansel, who is definitely not Jonah, holds up his palm for a high five. Seriously? He totally stole that from the real Jonah!

My dad slaps him five.

The real Jonah grumbles.

"This is the best spinach ever," fake Jonah says. He looks totally serious, too. I watch Hansel — happily — eat another forkful of the green stuff.

"Wow," my mom exclaims. "You two sure know how to make up for bad behavior. I've practically forgotten all about the broken lamp from last night. You came home from school, did your chores, and did your homework without being prompted. And now you're eating your veggies. I'm impressed."

"Does that mean I can have my golden ball back?" fake Jonah asks.

The real Jonah's eyes go huge, and his face scrunches up. Is Hansel trying to get his hands on my brother's prized ball? The one he told him all about?

"Yes, Jonah," my mom says. "But no more playing ball in the house. Right?"

"Right!" Hansel and Gretel say together. "We promise."

Real Jonah's cheeks and ears turn all red the way they do when he's really, really mad about something. He's about to go charging into the kitchen.

I grab my brother's arm. "We can't let Mom and Dad see us yet," I whisper. "They'll totally freak out."

Jonah's face is still scrunched up. "But Hansel is stealing my stuff!"

"We'll stop them," I whisper-promise.

"Does anyone want more salad?" Mom asks, lifting up the polka-dot bowl. "Oh, no, the salad bowl has a chip in it! How did that happen?"

I watch Gretel take some more lettuce. Then she eats

her final bite of steak. She dabs her mouth politely with her napkin.

Wait a minute. WAIT A MINUTE. Is Gretel wearing my FRA necklace? The one I made with my BFFs? She is! HEY!

"May I have more steak?" Gretel asks my mom. "It's sooo good."

"Of course, Abby," my mom says, beaming at her children.

Who are *not* her children.

OMG. Hansel and Gretel have been pretending to be us all day!

And they're really, really good at it.

How are we supposed to get our lives back?

"Who wants some fruit?" my dad asks.

Hansel yawns.

"Tired?" Mom asks.

Yeah, he's exhausted from pretending to be my brother all day.

Hansel nods. "You can make my bedtime an hour earlier if you think I could use the extra sleep on school nights," Hansel says as my dad hands him a bowl of fruit.

Jonah's cheeks and ears turn even redder.

"WHAT?!" Jonah whisper-yells. "NO WAY AM I GOING TO BED AN HOUR EARLIER. That's it, Abby, I'm going in there and telling them —"

"No," I whisper-yell back. "Not yet!"

"That is very mature of you, Jonah," my mother says to Hansel, winking at my dad.

Gretel smiles and pops a piece of cantaloupe in her mouth. "Frankie and Robin and I decided we're all going to wear orange tomorrow," Gretel says. "And Penny thinks it would be SO cute if we all wear pigtails, so we are."

Now *my* cheeks and ears are steaming red. Gretel is stealing my friends now? She must have been hanging out with Robin and Frankie all day. In my FRA necklace.

And there is no way I'm wearing pigtails tomorrow. NO. WAY.

"Okay, that's it!" I say, ready to charge in and tell our parents that the Abby and Jonah sitting at the table are impostors.

But now Jonah holds *me* back.

"Abby, we can't go in!" Jonah says. "Like you said, Mom and Dad will freak. How would we explain that there are two Abbys and two Jonahs? We'd have to tell them everything. And we can't!"

Crumbs. He's right.

"I'm so glad you're wearing that sweater Nana bought you, Jonah," my dad says to Hansel. "I thought you didn't like it."

Real Jonah's face scrunches up again. "I don't. It's itchy," he whispers.

I bet I know why Hansel put on that sweater. Because it's so bulky it makes him look less scrawny.

"What boy wouldn't like a cardigan sweater with little sailboats on it?" Hansel asks.

He looks totally serious, too.

Then again, it's probably the first warm sweater he's ever had on. Which makes me feel a little bad.

But Hansel and Gretel *are* trying to steal our lives. We have to do something to get those lives back.

Dad laughs. "Who are you two and what did you do with our children?"

Seriously?

Ruff! Ruff-ruff!

Oh, no! Prince is barking like crazy. He runs past us right into the kitchen.

He's sitting right behind Gretel's chair and going nuts.

"There you are, Prince!" my mom says. "We were looking for you all day. We almost sent out a search party."

Oh, sure, for *him* they were going to send out a search party. I bet they would have used a great photo for *him*.

Ruff! Ruff-ruff! Prince barks even louder, and runs over to Hansel. He keeps barking.

"That's enough, Prince!" my dad says. "I know you're excited to see Abby and Jonah now that you're back from wherever you ran off to. But no more barking."

Prince lets out one more tiny *ruff,* then drops down with a scowl. He's keeping his eye on Hansel and Gretel, though. Good dog.

"Come on, Jonah," I whisper. "Let's go hide upstairs in our rooms. We'll confront our impostors when they come up. If anyone is going to wear orange tomorrow, it's going to be me."

"And if anyone is wearing that ugly, itchy sweater, it's going to be me," Jonah whispers back.

I raise an eyebrow.

Jonah wrinkles his nose. "Fine, he can keep the sweater."

chapter sixteen

We Like Being Us

I go into my room, expecting to see that Gretel has turned it into HER room. But nothing is different. All my stuff is exactly where I left it.

I run to my jewelry box. Yesterday, Hansel and Gretel were on there, snacking on the witch's candy house. Now, though, they're eating dinner . . . at my kitchen table!

No. No way. This is not their happy ending.

They are not stealing my life. I'm putting a stop to it pronto.

But I can't just jump on them. I sneak over to Jonah's room and tell him to hide in his closet until they come upstairs.

I change into dry clothes and then I squeeze into my closet, beside my extra shoes.

Hmm. It's dark in here.

This closet could use a window. And maybe some snacks. A mini-fridge would be good. Perhaps a water fountain?

Finally, finally, finally, the door to my room opens.

"Hello, beautiful room," I hear Gretel say. "Hello, soft bed. Hello, thick pillow. And hello, fluffy rug." I hear a sigh. "Abby is so lucky."

I pop out of the closet.

"You!" she shrieks.

"Oh, yeah," I say, my hands on my hips. "It's me. And I'm not very happy with *you*."

A moment later, Jonah marches Hansel into my room. Hansel's cheeks are bright pink.

"Care to apologize for stealing our lives?" I ask.

"We couldn't help it," Gretel says. "The portal was swirling right in front of us."

Hansel digs his big toe into the carpet. "And you guys just kept bragging and bragging about how good you had it. With your school and your vegetables and your golden balls."

"But that wasn't fair!" I say. "The witch caught us!"

Gretel frowns. "She came back?"

"Yes!" I say. "And she took us prisoner in her house!"

"Well, so what?" Hansel says. "Otherwise she would have taken us prisoner!"

Fair point. "Maybe," I say. "But that doesn't excuse you for running away and stealing our lives."

"Sorry," Gretel says, her face crumpling. "I didn't know the witch was home."

"Me neither," Hansel says. "Sorry. But you got away, right? You're here."

"Yes," I say. "We got away. Barely. But we did."

"Then once again you're luckier than we are. You're back with your perfect family. And we still have nowhere to go," Gretel says with a sad frown.

"That's not true," Jonah says. "We saw your dad. He misses you and wants you to come home."

"I don't believe you," Gretel says suspiciously.

"It's true," I say. "Your stepmom is gone, and the witch and her bird are going to jail. And veggies will be available to every-one in Vegetopia."

"And your dad has a new girlfriend," Jonah adds. "She has a slingshot!"

"Huh?" they ask.

"Not important," I say with a wave of my hand. "But it's definitely safe to go home."

"Thanks," Gretel says. "We really are sorry we pretended to be you. But it was fun. School was fun! And your friends are nice. I really like Penny. I volunteered the two of us to clean out the fish tank tomorrow at recess."

Huh? "What? Penny? Recess?"

"The teacher asked for two volunteers to clean the fish tank, so I volunteered me and Penny! It's a mess. I thought it would be nice for Penny and me to spend some quality time together."

"Um . . ." I'm speechless.

"Oh, and you had a surprise math test today," Gretel says. "You did not know most of the answers unfortunately. Sorry."

Great. Just great. "Do I have any homework?" I spit out.

"Not that much," she says. "Although Ms. Masserman said I have something called detention."

What?! Detention? I've never had detention. EVER! "For what?"

"I'm not sure exactly. She kept telling me I had to raise my hand to talk, which I told her was absolutely ridiculous. Who raises their hand to talk? Their head maybe, but hand? I don't talk with my hands!"

I take a deep breath. A very, very deep breath. "Don't worry about it."

"I wasn't," she says with a shrug.

Hmph.

"I kind of have something of yours," Hansel says sheepishly.

"What?" Jonah asks nervously. I don't blame him for being nervous after hearing what Gretel did to *my* life.

Hansel reaches into the sailboat-dotted cardigan and pulls out Jonah's golden ball. "Your mom gave it to me. For eating so much spinach. And saying 'thank you' a lot."

Jonah takes the ball and holds it close to him. Then he takes a deep breath . . . and tosses it back to Hansel. "You can keep it."

"Really?"

Really?

"Really," Jonah says. "It probably belongs on your side of the mirror. It keeps breaking things on this side."

"It only broke one lamp," I say.

"And the polka-dot salad bowl," Jonah says with a laugh. "That's how it got chipped. Oh, and maybe a glass figurine or two. It doesn't matter. Not important!"

"So how do we get home?" Gretel asks, looking around the room. "Is there another swirly purple tree in your room that will take us back? Or do we go through your window, maybe?"

After everything they put us through, I'm tempted to tell them to try jumping out the window, but I don't. "There's a magic mirror in our basement," I say. "The one you came through."

"Hey," Jonah asks. "Did you guys meet Maryrose? The magic fairy in the mirror?"

"No," Gretel says. "We came through the mirror, landed in the basement, and just kind of walked around until we figured out which were your rooms. I can't believe this entire house is yours."

It's true. It *is* a pretty great place to live. I guess I've really been taking it for granted.

"Well, you two have to get home now," I say. "Your dad really misses you. He's waiting for you at the police station. Do you know where that is?"

Gretel nods. "We have to cross a big pond to get there, but I know the way."

"We can take Ms. Duck across," Hansel tells her.

"Yeah, just don't tell her to duck if you don't want Gretel to get mad," Jonah whispers with a grin.

"Huh?" Gretel asks.

"Nothing. Let's go down to the mirror," I say. "I'm sure Maryrose will let you through when we explain what happened."

"But it's not midnight," Jonah says. "The mirror only works at midnight."

"We have to try," I say.

I tiptoe out of my bedroom and look up and down the hallway. No sign of my parents. Good. I head back in my room and close the door.

"Jonah," I say, "go downstairs and make sure Mom and Dad aren't around. I'm going to sneak Hansel and Gretel to the basement. If you hear Mom and Dad, make sure they don't see us!"

"Got it," he says.

"Abby?" Gretel asks, biting her lip.

"Yeah?" I say.

"Can I keep this outfit?" she asks. She glances down at my red sweater and jeans. She's even wearing my purple high-tops.

"Sure," I say. Not the first time I've lost clothes to a fairy tale.

"You can keep the sweater," Jonah tells Hansel. "I hate that thing. It's so ugly."

Hansel frowns. "This sweater? No, thanks. It *is* really ugly!"

Jonah sighs as Hansel takes off the sweater and hands it to him.

"You should probably have this back, too," Gretel says, removing the FRA necklace and handing it to me.

"Thanks," I say, and put it around my neck. "I appreciate you giving it back. Okay, Jonah — go be the lookout." I turn to Hansel and Gretel. "Come on, guys. Time to go."

We slip downstairs. I hear my parents in the kitchen. Please don't come out and see two Abbys and two Jonahs!

"Hurry!" I whisper as we round the corner to the basement door.

Success — our parents don't come out of the kitchen.

We rush down the steps and stop in front of the mirror.

I knock three times.

Nothing happens.

"Maryrose?" I call. "Hello? It's me, Abby."

"And Jonah!" he says.

"And Hansel and Gretel," Hansel adds.

"Maryrose?" I say again, knocking three more times. "Hansel and Gretel need to go home. I know it's not midnight, but can you open the portal so they can leave?"

No answer.

Crumbs.

"I guess we really do have to wait till midnight," I say. "Okay, everyone back upstairs. Quietly!"

We all head back up to my room.

So much for getting my life back.

"Abby? Jonah?" my parents call. "Do you want to come watch a show with us in the den?"

I'm about to tell Hansel and Gretel that it's their turn to hide in the closet, when I change my mind.

"Go ahead," I say. "Have you ever watched TV?"

"Yeah," she says. "Today after school. How do those people get in there anyway? How does it work?"

I laugh. "I have no idea," I admit.

She shakes her head. "I'm sure you want to see your parents. You go. Really. I'm happy to take a nap in your bed. So soft! Like sleeping on clouds. And this pillow," she says with a sigh, leaning her head against it. "Like a marshmallow. I don't have a pillow of my own. Just a bale of hay in an old dress that I put under my head."

A bale of hay? Like in the cottage? That's horrible. I suddenly feel *really* bad about all the complaining I did yesterday.

"Well, get some rest," I say. "I'll keep my mom out. I'll wake you at midnight."

I quickly change into pj's, say good night, and tuck her in. As I look around my room at all my stuff, I realize how much I really have. And not just the basic stuff like pillows and a comfy bed and warm clothes. I have a nice house. Great parents. A teacher who cares how I do on tests. Friends. I have all that and so many extras. Like a family laptop and iPad. My amazing watch. And how many pairs of shoes do I have in my closet? A lot.

I run down to see my parents.

"Hi!" I call out, jumping in between them. I give them a big hug. "I love you guys. Have I told you that lately? You're the best."

"What's up with you two today?" my mom asks, looking between me and Jonah. "It's like aliens possessed my kids!"

"Don't jinx it," my dad says. "I like it."

Jonah is already sitting on the couch. He gives me a wink.

At least I think it's Jonah.

I'm ninety-nine percent sure.

"I think I'm still hungry," my dad says. "Should I get us something sweet? Chocolate-chip cookies maybe?"

Jonah and I look at each other. We've had a lot of sugar in the last twenty-four hours. A LOT.

I shrug. "There's always room for a snack."

My alarm goes off at eleven fifty. I slept on the floor and let Gretel sleep in my bed. I'm nice like that.

I shake Gretel awake. She yawns and stands up. "Time to go?" she asks.

149

"Yup," I say. "Let's go wake up our little brothers."

We sneak into Jonah's room. Jonah is in his bed, and Hansel is sleeping on the floor — I guess Jonah is not as nice as I am. Or Hansel likes sleeping on the floor. I wake up Jonah, and Gretel wakes up Hansel.

Both boys have the same funny bedhead.

"Be right back," I say, and rush into my room. I grab the big box from under my bed and carry it into the hallway.

"What's in the box?" Gretel asks as we head downstairs and then go down the final flight of stairs to the basement.

"You'll see," Jonah says. "Abby and I put together a big care package for you and Hansel."

I packed cheese and crackers, fruit, two boxes of spaghetti, and two adorable reusable water bottles. Plus toys, books, pillows, and blankets. Also the rest of the chocolate-chip cookies. Jonah tried to sneak one when we were packing up the box, but I slapped his hand away. How many times does he want to throw up in one day?

"It's thirty seconds to midnight," I say. "Ready, you two?"

Ruff! Prince barks.

"Not you, Prince," I say. "We're not going. Just Hansel and Gretel."

"We'll miss you guys," Gretel says. "Thanks for everything."

The four of us stand in front of the mirror, looking at our four reflections. It's amazing how identical we look. Who would ever have guessed that Jonah and I would find our look-alikes in fairy land?

Jonah knocks on the mirror. Then again. Then a third time.

The mirror starts to swirl. Jonah and Prince and I stand to the side so we don't get sucked in.

"Bye!" Hansel and Gretel say as Gretel clutches the box tight against her chest.

"Bye!" Jonah and I say.

"One, two . . . three!" Gretel counts.

Then she and Hansel jump through the mirror.

When the mirror clears and we see our reflections again, I call out, "Maryrose? Are you there?"

The mirror ripples. I see the very faint image of a woman's face in the glass. Her long hair flows down along the side of the mirror.

She's there!

"Of course I'm here," she says.

I have so many questions! "Hi! Don't go! I have to ask you stuff!"

"Go ahead," she says.

Okay! "Did you think Hansel and Gretel were us?" I ask. "Is that why you let them through the mirror into our basement?"

"Absolutely not," Maryrose says with a laugh. "I knew what I was doing."

"Why, then?" Jonah asks.

"Did you learn something by being in their world?" Maryrose asks.

"Yes," I say.

"What?"

"That we were being spoiled brats," Jonah says.

She laughs again. "Exactly."

My cheeks heat up, but I keep going. "Did you know they looked just like us?"

Maryrose smiles. "Of course. That's one of the reasons I chose you. You reminded me of them."

"Huh?" I say. "Chose us? You *chose* us? But you couldn't have! The mirror was here when we moved in! Didn't we choose you?"

She laughs a third time. "No, little ones. I definitely chose you."

My heart speeds up.

"But for what?" Jonah asks. "For the mission?"

"Yes," she says. "Absolutely."

"But what's the mission?"

Instead of answering, Maryrose slowly fades away.

"Wait! Maryrose!" I say.

The mirror ripples until it's smooth again.

"Aww," Jonah and I both say.

I have so many more questions. Next time. I'll have to ask her next time.

Jonah, Prince, and I climb back upstairs. I give them each a hug good night and then close my door.

I sneak a final peek at my jewelry box. Hansel and Gretel are by the pond with their dad, sitting on one of the blankets I gave them and having a picnic. Ms. Duck is floating on the pond. Hansel is taking a bite out of a cookie.

They look happy.

chapter seventeen

We're Us Again!

In the morning, my alarm goes off, and I bounce out of bed.

Jonah comes out of his room with his usual messy bed-head, and we go downstairs.

My mom is still in her bathrobe. "Smoothie?" she asks.

Jonah and I give each other horrified looks.

I swallow. Hard. "Sure," I say. "Thanks, Mom."

"My pleasure!" she says.

Jonah whispers to me, "Do we have to drink them?"

Yes! I mouth back. *Be grateful for the smoothie! Be grateful for Mom!* "You know what?" I say to Mom. "I can make them."

"Yeah?" she asks, surprised. "You know how? When did you learn?"

"Oh . . . by watching you!" I say, which is basically true. "You can get ready for work. I'll call you when they're done."

"Sure," she says, stepping back. "Thanks!"

"I'll take care of the bagels," Jonah says just as my dad is about to pop the bagels in the toaster oven.

"Sounds good to me," my dad says. "I'll pour the coffee. For me and your mom. Not for you."

"Obviously," I say. Anyway, coffee is disgusting. But not as disgusting as black licorice.

"Thanks, kids," my mom says. "We appreciate the help."

"We appreciate you," I say.

I pop a banana, some blueberries, milk, yogurt, and some ice in the blender. I see leftovers of last night's spinach in a Ziploc container. I throw in a piece for good luck.

I press BLEND and hope for the best.

155

acknowledgments

Thank you to all the publishing people who turn my ingredients into a book:

Aimee Friedman, Laura Dail, Tamar Rydzinski, Lauren Walters, Deb Shapiro, Jennifer Abbots, Olivia Valcarce, Abby McAden, David Levithan, Tracy van Straaten, Caitlin Friedman, Rachel Feld, Antonio Gonzalez, Sue Flynn and everyone in Sales, Rachael Hicks, Emily Rader, Elizabeth Parisi, Lizette Serrano, Emily Heddleson, and Robin Bailey Hoffman, and everyone in the school channels!

Thank you, family, friends, writers, and others: Elissa Ambrose, Aviva Mlynowski, Larry Mlynowski, Louisa Weiss, Robert Ambrose, the Dalven-Swidlers, the DAttilios, the Goldmiths, the Heckers, the Finkelstein-Mitchells, the Steins, the Wolfes, the Mittlemans, the Bilermans, the Greens, Courtney Sheinmel, Anne Heltzel, Lauren Myracle, Emily Bender, Targia Alphonse, Jess Braun, Lauren Kisilevsky, Bonnie Altro, Carolyn Mackler, Caroline Gertler, Stuart Gibbs, Jen E. Smith, Robin Wasserman, Adele Griffin, Leslie Margolis, Maryrose Wood, Tara Altebrando, Sara

Zarr, Ally Carter, Jennifer Barnes, Alan Gratz, Penny Fransblow, Avery Carmichael, Maggie Marr, Jeremy Cammy, and Farrin Jacobs. Also, my special readers, Priya DAttilio, Sofie Dewan, and, of course, Chloe Swidler.

Thank you, Todd, and my Chloe and Anabelle — I love you even more than chocolate peanut butter cups, cookie dough ice cream, and salted caramel. Mwah!

Thank you, readers: You guys are the sweetest.

Robin squeals.

"What?" Penny and I ask at the same time.

"I . . . I . . ." Robin's face pinches together. And I realize — she's shrinking! Oh my goodness. She's like a balloon that's losing air. I watch in disbelief as my friend gets smaller and smaller. Her arms are flailing. She's three feet. Two feet. Is she ever going to stop? What if she disappears?

Finally, the shrinking comes to an end. My best friend Robin is now about the size of a pencil. Her hands are the size of erasers. She's a miniature Robin, with a tiny reddish ponytail, a tiny orange shirt, tiny blue jeans, tiny sneakers, a tiny FRA necklace, and teeny, tiny freckles.

THIS IS SO WEIRD.

Robin screams. It's a super high-pitched scream like she just inhaled helium.

"Robin is tiny!" Penny shrieks.

"Teeny tiny!" I add.

Penny shakes her head back and forth and back and forth. "IT WORKED. IT'S REALLY A SHRINKING POTION. Ahhhh! Does that mean . . . does that mean we're really in *Alice's Adventures in Wonderland*? We're really IN a book?"

"Seems that way," I say. I can hardly believe it, either. Even after all my fairy tale experience.

I look down at my minuscule friend. "Are you okay, Robin?" I ask.

"I'm better than okay," Tiny Robin chirps. "I'm terrific. That was the coolest thing ever! I'm itty-bitty! Woo-hoo! The potion was real!"

I laugh. Magic is amazing.

"I just can't believe it," Penny says. She kneels down to examine the newly pencil-sized Robin.

I eye the bottle. "What does it taste like?" I ask.

"Like Orange Crush," Tiny Robin replies. "Fizzy but fruity."

"Are we really going to drink it?" Penny asks, standing back up. "Maybe we shouldn't. Who knows what can happen?"

"We're going to get small," I say. I *am* a little nervous. I've turned into a beast and a mouse, flown on a magic carpet, and breathed underwater, among other things. But I've never been tiny.

"Just drink the potion already!" Tiny Robin cries. "C'mon, guys! Turn small and we'll go into the garden to look for Frankie. And then we can go to the tea party, too. All those little finger sandwiches. Delish!"

My stomach growls. I am hungry. We never did get to have the spaghetti that Penny's nanny was making.

"Do you want me to go first?" I ask Penny.

Penny bites her lip. "*A* does come before *P* alphabetically."

I never realized Penny was so . . . wimpy. Maybe she's just freaked out. I would be, too, if I had never traveled to fairy tale realms.

"Okay," I say. "Here goes nothing." I lift up the bottle and sniff it — and wrinkle my nose. It smells gross. I take a sip. Blech. Orange soda? More like a dirt-and-leaf smoothie.

I quickly swallow some of it down. And wait.

And . . . hey! I'm shriiiiinnnnkkking! My legs are getting shorter. And now my arms. My body is going down, down, down. Now my head and neck are following. The rest of the world is getting bigger as I get smaller.

Eeeeep!

Then the shrinking stops. I stare down at myself. I'm pencil–sized. So are my clothes.

I have to admit, shrinking *was* cool.

"Welcome!" Tiny Robin cries, giving me a tiny high five. We're exactly the same size now. Does that make me Tiny Abby?

The hallway around us looks huge. The glass table looks massive. And Penny looks like a giant.

Ahhhh! Giant Penny! She could squash me with her sneaker in one giant step.

"I'm not sure I want to do this," Penny says, her giant hands shaking.

"Penny, you promised," Robin says. "We have to find Frankie!"

"You don't have to shrink," I say quickly. "You can stay here and wait for us to come back." To be honest, I'd much rather be on this adventure with just Robin.

Penny narrows her eyes, apparently reading my mind. "Sure. And let you have all the fun with Robin without me? I don't think so."

I watch her take a sip of the potion.

In seconds, she's shrinking down, down, down, until she's pencil-sized like us.

Tiny Penny looks down at herself and shrieks. Then she squares her shoulder and lifts her chin. "Ready," she declares.

Robin pushes open the door to outside. She runs out first. I go next, and I fit through easily. Penny follows me out, and the door slams shut behind us.

We're in the garden.

Each time Abby and Jonah get sucked into their magic mirror, they wind up in a different fairy tale — and find new adventures!

Read all the Whatever After books!

Whatever After #1: FAIREST of ALL

In their first adventure, Abby and Jonah wind up in the story of *Snow White*. But when they stop Snow from eating the poisoned apple, they realize they've messed up the whole story! Can they fix it — and still find Snow her happy ending?

Whatever After #2: IF the SHOE FITS

This time, Abby and Jonah find themselves in Cinderella's story. When Cinderella breaks her foot, the glass slipper won't fit! With a little bit of magic, quick thinking, and luck, can Abby and her brother save the day?

Whatever After #3: SINK or SWIM

Abby and Jonah are pulled into the tale of *The Little Mermaid* — a story with an ending that is *not* happy. So Abby and Jonah mess it up on purpose! Can they convince the mermaid to keep her tail before it's too late?

Whatever After #4: DREAM ON

Now Abby and Jonah are lost in Sleeping Beauty's story, along with Abby's friend Robin. Before they know it, Sleeping Beauty is wide awake and Robin is fast asleep. How will Abby and Jonah make things right?

Whatever After #5: BAD HAIR DAY

When Abby and Jonah fall into Rapunzel's story, they mess everything up by giving Rapunzel a haircut! Can they untangle this fairy tale disaster in time?

Whatever After #6: COLD AS ICE

When their dog, Prince, runs through the mirror, Abby and Jonah have no choice but to follow him into the story of *The Snow Queen*! It's a winter wonderland . . . but the Snow Queen is rather mean, and she FREEZES Prince! Can Abby and Jonah save their dog . . . and themselves?

Whatever After #7: BEAUTY QUEEN

This time, Abby and Jonah fall into the story of *Beauty and the Beast*. When Jonah is the one taken prisoner instead of Beauty, Abby has to find a way to fix this fairy tale . . . before things get pretty ugly!

Whatever After #8: ONCE *upon* a FROG

When Abby and Jonah fall into the fairy tale of *The Frog Prince*, they realize the princess is so rude they don't even *want* her help! But will they be able to figure out how to turn the frog back into a prince all by themselves?

Whatever After #9: GENIE in a BOTTLE

The mirror has dropped Abby and Jonah into the story of *Aladdin*! When things go wrong with the genie, the siblings have to escape an enchanted cave, learn to fly a magic carpet, and figure out WHAT to wish for . . . so they can help Aladdin *and* get back home!

Whatever After #10: SUGAR and SPICE

When Abby and Jonah get mixed up in Hansel and Gretel's story, they're the ones who end up trapped in the witch's cake house! Can the siblings avoid getting eaten, put everything right, and make it back to home sweet home?

Whatever After #11:
TWO PEAS in a POD

Abby is mistaken for the princess when she and Jonah land in *The Princess and the Pea*. She may love the royal treatment, but can a princess contest find the kingdom a true leader?

Whatever After SPECIAL EDITION:
ABBY in WONDERLAND

Abby and her friends fall down the rabbit hole into *Alice's Adventures in Wonderland*! Can they solve the Cheshire Cat's riddle, make it through a wacky tea party with the Mad Hatter, and escape the terrible Queen of Hearts?

WHAT HAPPEN
YOUR MAGIC
UPSIDE DO

From bestselling authors
Sarah Mlynowski, Lauren Myracle,
and **Emily Jenkins** comes a series about
magical misfits who don't fit in at their school.